Our Clever Corbies

Danielle Ackley-McPhail

James Chambers

Doc Coleman

Ef Deal

Judi Fleming

Dana Fraedrich

Jessica Lucci

Aaron Rosenberg

Michelle D. Sonnier

David Lee Summers

Levi Leland and Virginia Poe

Steampunk titles by eSpec Books

THE CLOCKWORK CHRONICLES
The Clockwork Witch
The Clockwork Solution
(Michelle D. Sonnier)

Baba Ali and the Clockwork Djinn
(Danielle Ackley-McPhail
and Day Al-Mohamed)

A Curse of Ash and Iron
(Christine Norris)

Spirit Seeker
(Jeff Young)

Esprit De Corpse
(Ef Deal)

Crimson Whisper
(Ken Schrader)

Steampunk Anthologies by eSpec Books

After Punk:
Steampowered tales of the Afterlife

Gaslight & Grimm
Grimm Machinations

Grease Monkeys:
The Heart and Soul of Dieselpunk

The Weird Wild West

FORGOTTEN LORE
VOLUME ONE

A CAST OF CROWS

EDITED BY
DANIELLE ACKLEY-McPHAIL

NEOPARADOXA
Pennsville, NJ

PUBLISHED BY
NeoParadoxa,
a division of eSpec Books LLC
Danielle McPhail,
Publisher
PO Box 242,
Pennsville, New Jersey 08070
www.especbooks.com

ISBN: 978-1-956463-19-4
ISBN (ebook): 978-1-956463-18-7

Cover and Interior Design: Danielle McPhail, McP Digital Graphics

Illustrations:
Art Credits - www.Shutterstock.com
clipping photo crows © Egor Design
Dead cliff road on the dead mysterious forest with three crows on the
night © bluefish_ds
The plague doctor points to a gray background © YuriyZhuravov
Steampunk metallic frame with copper clockwork gears and blue
banner isolated on black 3D digital © T Studio
raven and skull © alexblacksea

For all of those who fly in the face
of Nevermore.

THE RAVEN

EDGAR ALLAN POE

Once upon a midnight dreary, while I pondered, weak and weary,
Over many a quaint and curious volume of forgotten lore —
While I nodded, nearly napping, suddenly there came a tapping,
As of some one gently rapping, rapping at my chamber door.
"'Tis some visitor," I muttered, "tapping at my chamber door —
Only this and nothing more."

Ah, distinctly I remember it was in the bleak December;
And each separate dying ember wrought its ghost upon the floor.
Eagerly I wished the morrow; — vainly I had sought to borrow
From my books surcease of sorrow — sorrow for the lost Lenore —
For the rare and radiant maiden whom the angels name Lenore —
Nameless here for evermore.

And the silken, sad, uncertain rustling of each purple curtain
Thrilled me — filled me with fantastic terrors never felt before;
So that now, to still the beating of my heart, I stood repeating
"'Tis some visitor entreating entrance at my chamber door —
Some late visitor entreating entrance at my chamber door; —
This it is and nothing more."

Presently my soul grew stronger; hesitating then no longer,
"Sir," said I, "or Madam, truly your forgiveness I implore;
But the fact is I was napping, and so gently you came rapping,
And so faintly you came tapping, tapping at my chamber door,
That I scarce was sure I heard you" — here I opened wide the door; —
Darkness there and nothing more.

Deep into that darkness peering, long I stood there wondering, fearing,
Doubting, dreaming dreams no mortal ever dared to dream before;
But the silence was unbroken, and the stillness gave no token,
And the only word there spoken was the whispered word, "Lenore?"
This I whispered, and an echo murmured back the word, "Lenore!" —
Merely this and nothing more.

Back into the chamber turning, all my soul within me burning,
Soon again I heard a tapping somewhat louder than before.
"Surely," said I, "surely that is something at my window lattice;
Let me see, then, what thereat is, and this mystery explore —
Let my heart be still a moment and this mystery explore; —
'Tis the wind and nothing more!"

Open here I flung the shutter, when, with many a flirt and flutter,
In there stepped a stately Raven of the saintly days of yore;
Not the least obeisance made he; not a minute stopped or stayed he;
But, with mien of lord or lady, perched above my chamber door —
Perched upon a bust of Pallas just above my chamber door —
Perched, and sat, and nothing more.

Then this ebony bird beguiling my sad fancy into smiling,
By the grave and stern decorum of the countenance it wore,
"Though thy crest be shorn and shaven, thou," I said, "art sure no craven,
Ghastly grim and ancient Raven wandering from the Nightly shore —
Tell me what thy lordly name is on the Night's Plutonian shore!"
Quoth the Raven "Nevermore."

Much I marvelled this ungainly fowl to hear discourse so plainly,
Though its answer little meaning — little relevancy bore;
For we cannot help agreeing that no living human being
Ever yet was blessed with seeing bird above his chamber door —
Bird or beast upon the sculptured bust above his chamber door,
With such name as "Nevermore."

But the Raven, sitting lonely on the placid bust, spoke only
That one word, as if his soul in that one word he did outpour.
Nothing farther then he uttered — not a feather then he fluttered —
Till I scarcely more than muttered "Other friends have flown before —
On the morrow he will leave me, as my Hopes have flown before."
Then the bird said "Nevermore."

Startled at the stillness broken by reply so aptly spoken,
"Doubtless," said I, "what it utters is its only stock and store
Caught from some unhappy master whom unmerciful Disaster
Followed fast and followed faster till his songs one burden bore —
Till the dirges of his Hope that melancholy burden bore
Of 'Never — nevermore'."

But the Raven still beguiling all my fancy into smiling,
Straight I wheeled a cushioned seat in front of bird, and bust and door;
Then, upon the velvet sinking, I betook myself to linking
Fancy unto fancy, thinking what this ominous bird of yore —
What this grim, ungainly, ghastly, gaunt, and ominous bird of yore
Meant in croaking "Nevermore."

This I sat engaged in guessing, but no syllable expressing
To the fowl whose fiery eyes now burned into my bosom's core;
This and more I sat divining, with my head at ease reclining
On the cushion's velvet lining that the lamp-light gloated o'er,
But whose velvet-violet lining with the lamp-light gloating o'er,
She shall press, ah, nevermore!

Then, methought, the air grew denser, perfumed from an unseen censer
Swung by Seraphim whose foot-falls tinkled on the tufted floor.
"Wretch," I cried, "thy God hath lent thee — by these angels he hath sent thee
Respite — respite and nepenthe from thy memories of Lenore;
Quaff, oh quaff this kind nepenthe and forget this lost Lenore!"
Quoth the Raven "Nevermore."

"Prophet!" said I, "thing of evil! — prophet still, if bird or devil! —
Whether Tempter sent, or whether tempest tossed thee here ashore,
Desolate yet all undaunted, on this desert land enchanted —
On this home by Horror haunted — tell me truly, I implore —
Is there — is there balm in Gilead? — tell me — tell me, I implore!"
Quoth the Raven "Nevermore."

"Prophet!" said I, "thing of evil! — prophet still, if bird or devil!
By that Heaven that bends above us — by that God we both adore —
Tell this soul with sorrow laden if, within the distant Aidenn,
It shall clasp a sainted maiden whom the angels name Lenore —
Clasp a rare and radiant maiden whom the angels name Lenore."
Quoth the Raven "Nevermore."

"Be that word our sign of parting, bird or fiend!" I shrieked, upstarting —
"Get thee back into the tempest and the Night's Plutonian shore!
Leave no black plume as a token of that lie thy soul hath spoken!
Leave my loneliness unbroken! — quit the bust above my door!
Take thy beak from out my heart, and take thy form from off my door!"
Quoth the Raven "Nevermore."

And the Raven, never flitting, still is sitting, still is sitting
On the pallid bust of Pallas just above my chamber door;
And his eyes have all the seeming of a demon's that is dreaming,
And the lamp-light o'er him streaming throws his shadow on the floor;
And my soul from out that shadow that lies floating on the floor
Shall be lifted — nevermore!

CONTENTS

A Master of Genres

THE NAME EDGAR ALLAN POE CONJURES UP THOUGHTS OF premature burial, gruesome murders, black cats, beating hearts, and ravens. As the master of the horror story and the godfather of goth, Poe will forever be synonymous with these haunting images. This Boston-born writer from the nineteenth century created much more than just the thrilling effects of psychological horror through his storytelling. Poe wrote about sea voyages, hot air balloon travel, mesmerism, and mystery. With his publication of "The Murders in the Rue Morgue" in 1841, Poe single handedly invented the mystery genre as we know it today. With his subsequent publications of "The Mystery of Marie Roget" and "The Purloined Letter," Poe created the various templates for every mystery story ever told: a detective solving a murder that had happened, a detective solving a murder that was happening, and a detective solving a murder happening somewhere else.

When we think of the science fiction genre, our minds might go to Jules Verne or H. G. Wells, but Poe was already being acknowledged as the inspiration such authors. Poe charted that previously uncharted territory, and left future writers to expound upon it. So, while Poe explored science, criticism, art, cryptography, and even interior decorating, he left us with no shortage of topics to appreciate. You can ask one hundred different people what they like about Poe and receive as many different answers. Poe's life was the biggest horror story of all, while his death was his most puzzling mystery. For these reasons, Poe always gains intrigue. Poe attracts an audience. His legacy is as tenacious as his crime-solving detective, C. Auguste Dupin. Edgar Allan Poe's inspiration has had a ripple effect on writers and artists throughout the centuries. He has brought together communities of people of varying interests through his creation of a universe flooded with genres. Not only is Poe credited with creating the very concept of genres, but he also is the root of inspiration for contemporary genres as well, such as Steampunk.

When you hear the term steampunk what do you think of? Most would say people in late 1800s fashion adorned with mechanical embellishments. Aesthetically speaking, this is true. But the fashion is only one part of this movement. While the concept of Steampunk is not new, the term was unintentionally coined in the late 1980s by writer K.W. Jeter. It was the word he used to describe the writing that he and his fellow contemporaries were working on at that time. Simply put, Victorian-level technology in a future that never happened. A world without oil, a world run by steam combustion. The alternate reality of steampunk appeals to many for having one foot in the past and one foot in the future.

So here we are, at the crossroads. This is the place where Poe and the world of Steampunk walk along the same cobblestone streets. Poe was not just a writer of the macabre, he was a pioneer in what would later be known as the horror genre. His work continues to influence artists, musicians, actors, directors, teachers, and writers even now, this very book being a prime example. He was a poet of love, loss, and wonder. He was commissioned to write essays. He was an editor and reviewed the writings of his contemporaries. And as we stated before, just look at what he did for the detective mystery genre. His formulas are still being used today and have been since just past his death. To say the very least, there is something for everyone in the writings of Poe. The very same can be said of Steampunk. Within these pages, both collide bringing readers hours of chilling enjoyment in the finest tradition of the master.

Poetically Yours,
Levi Leland & Virginia Poe
Hosts of Beyond The Oblong Box Podcast

A Heavy Air

Aaron Rosenberg

ANY PARTY ABOARD AN AIRSHIP WAS CONSIDERED A FINE affair, and the *Prospero* was widely held to be the finest airship in existence. Thus, Phillipe Huron reasoned, this night could reasonably be expected to be the crème de la crème.

And yet, as he surveyed the grand ballroom, its rarefied air already stirred by the passage of many silent, black-clad staff flitting about making final preparations, he felt little joy at the prospect before him.

"Too many people!" Detective Dupin declared from his shoulder, and Phillipe absently reached up to stroke the bird's sable head, just above its beak.

"Yes, there will certainly be too many," he agreed, still studying the room. "Let us hope that all of them have only frivolity on their minds."

"Sir?" one of the officers asked, but Phillipe waved him away, then sighed and turned to the man instead.

"Has everything been checked?" he asked, and the blue-clad officer — Lloyd Lively — straightened.

"Yes, Inspector!" he announced with all the tedious enthusiasm of the young and bold. "Every inch checked, every guest confirmed against the list!"

Phillipe resisted the urge to sigh. "And Mister Travers?"

"Safe and sound, sir!" Lively declared. "As is his lady wife. But Miss Stevens apparently has a headache, so she'll not be greeting guests with him initially."

"Very well." Phillipe gave the room one final look. So many cabinets to duck into, so many nooks and crannies to lurk within, so many doors and mirrors to confuse the eye! He didn't like it one bit, despite its sumptuous carpeting and satin-covered walls, its crystal chandeliers and elaborately carved fireplaces. No, give him a small, plain room with one entrance and one exit any day.

But of course, that would not have provided Daniel Richard Travers with the pomp and circumstance he required. Phillipe had tried reasoning with the man. When one worried for one's life, one did not throw a massive party—and a costume party at that! Everyone's identity concealed as a matter of course! To do so was asking for trouble.

Sadly, as per usual, there was no reasoning with the rich and powerful. And Travers was both. "I'm not going to live in fear, Inspector," he'd said with a dismissive laugh. "If the threats are real, well, that's why you're here, isn't it?"

It was. Phillipe just hoped that would be enough.

He nodded to Lively, who gestured to Harris, who waved to Racine, who tapped on the heavily inlaid panels of a small door set at the back of the ballroom. This would have been far easier if they could have communicated via wireless, but of course a zeppelin's machinery was so delicate, no other devices were allowed onboard for fear of upsetting that balance. So old-school it was.

The door creaked open, and a man emerged, flanked by two more officers. He was neither tall nor short, fat nor thin. His black shirt and pants, gloves and boots, were similar to those worn by his staff, though of finer fabric and a more precise cut, but the broad-brimmed black leather hat, short satin cape, and silver rapier at his side set him apart. That and the almost palpable air of power he exuded, an aura of wealth and authority wrapped more tightly than any cloak.

"Are we ready, then?" Travers asked, adjusting his mask, which covered only his eyes and the bridge of his nose. It wouldn't do to conceal that famously toothy smile, after all! "Excellent!" The lawyer and financier clapped his hands together, and two servants stepped forward to pull back the wide double doors of the main entrance, allowing the guests to begin flowing in.

Their host stood waiting for them, placed to best advantage directly before the doors but far enough back that people had to enter the room fully to reach him. If he was annoyed that his personal secretary—the job as fine a fiction as any novel!—was not arrayed upon his arm in her usual decorative style, his manner did not show it, nor did his effusive greetings to his guests. He did not call any by name, of course, even in cases where their true identity was no better concealed than the sun behind a wisp of cloud, for that would shatter the illusion. Instead, he welcomed jester and clown, knight and sorcerer, rocketeer and airman.

Each and every one was known to him, of course. That was the advantage of holding a party aboard your private airship. The *Prospero* had cast off from its moorings a full two hours before, and Phillipe's men had combed every inch of it since.

The only people on board were those who had been specifically invited.

That did not prevent him from looking askance at some of the costumes, which were in poor taste or simply macabre humor. There was the Grim Reaper, for example, his dark robes spattered with what looked like blood and his mask that of an anguished, bloody corpse. There was the executioner, his dark hood blank save for two roughly cut eyeholes, his costume equal parts leather and buckles—and the axe over his shoulder nearly as tall as he was. There was the plague doctor, his long leather beak pointed and fierce, his hood pulled up over his head, his black trenchcoat both elegant and off-putting—Detective Dupin cawed in consternation at that one, seeing a beak longer than his own and round glass lenses more reflective than his own dark eyes.

Mrs. Travers stomped past, arrayed in handsome red velvet robes lined at the collar with ermine, a massive, elaborate white wig piled high atop her head and spilling in thick braids halfway down her back, diamonds glittering at brow and throat and ear. A Tsarina, Phillipe thought, clear testament to her role as the still powerful yet cast aside co-ruler. One man wore the tricorn hat and long blue coat of a revolutionary, white baldrics crossed over his chest, hair tied back in a black ribbon, flintlock rifle in his hand and cavalry saber at his side. That one bore watching, as did the half dozen others openly bearing weapons, real or otherwise.

Of course, Phillipe and his men received stares of their own, some appreciative and others disdainful, for they were all attired as a police inspector and his officers.

At least no one could accuse them of inaccuracy in their costumes!

As the ballroom filled, servers circulating with drinks and appetizers presented upon silver trays held aloft, it became harder and harder to pick individuals out of the crowd. Everywhere was an explosion of color, a cacophony of texture and pattern, a dizzying array of shapes and edges. The handful of darker costumes stood out, or at least the starker ones, such as the classic harlequin in her black and red checks. After the influx slowed, most of the guests now being present, Phillipe abandoned his original observation post by a fireplace midway along one wall and began a slow circuit of the space. Every dozen feet or two, the wall was broken by a set of curtained French doors leading into a small cabinet, those spaces furnished with bookcases and desks and couches and chairs, perfect for a private assignation or a moment of solitude. He peered in each one that was open but refrained from knocking on those that were closed, out of respect for people's privacy. He was here to protect, not to snoop.

In one such room, he saw the plague doctor. The man had taken possession of an armchair by the fire, a snifter of brandy upon the small table at his side, and seemed lost in contemplation of the flames, only twitching slightly at Phillipe's approach. With a small shudder, and a subvocalized caw from Dupin, he left the beaked man to his study and continued on.

A stir caused him to turn back toward the main doors in time to see a resplendent figure pause there, set off perfectly within the gilt doorframe. Her body-hugging gown was a shimmer of metallic golds and blues and greens that somehow gave the appearance of softness, like feathers, even though he suspected the fabric was in fact closer to scales. The garment left one shoulder and both arms bare, to be covered instead by long gloves patterned to resemble a peacock's plumage. Feathers did adorn her slender neck, in an elegant choker, and an elaborate headpiece shaped like a golden beak came down over her coiffed blond hair, covering forehead, eyes, and nose but leaving full lips and delicate chin exposed.

Miss Lorelei Stevens had arrived.

She strolled into the room as if she owned it, a fact Mrs. Travers frostily chose to ignore. But the radiant young lady's pleasure soon turned to confusion, as no dashing masked marauder arrived to extol her virtues and lead her around.

"Where is Daniel?" she asked someone, turning this way and that. "Daniel? Where are you?"

That jolted Phillipe from any appreciation of the scene, the setting, or the secretary, and he straightened, using his height to good advantage as he too searched for the man of the hour.

But Travers was nowhere to be found.

"Parkins! Whitmer!" The two officers made their way to him through the crowd, but the fact that they did not have a masked man in tow, and their own guilty expressions, already told the story. "What happened?"

Whitmer looked down at her feet. "Don't know, sir," she admitted, her voice scarcely heard over the crowd. "One minute he was right between us. Next we knew, a server tripped over a flamingo—a lady dressed like one, that is—who dumped her drink on a steamboat pilot, who fell against a priest and a devil. All Hell broke loose, and when I looked up, Mr. Travers was gone."

There was no point berating them, or bemoaning the incident. Instead, Phillipe focused on righting the wrong. "Find him," he ordered. "Now." Turning, he saw Lively across the room, but the officer did not see him. "Dupin," he said instead, his crow tilting its head to listen. "Tell Lively. All hands on deck. Find Travers." The bird cawed once and took flight, a sooty shadow arrowing above the crowd toward the clueless policeman. Phillipe knew he could count on his feathered companion to deliver the message accurately.

Within minutes, all his men were engaged in the search. They quartered the ballroom, then began working their way through each cabinet in turn. Even those closed doors were no longer allowed as an obstacle. Yet there was no sign of the man.

The plague doctor was still seated alone in his small room, and Phillipe risked disturbing the strange figure to ask, "Have you seen Mr. Travers?" When the man did not answer, he entered fully, Dupin back in place on his shoulder, approaching the armchair and its dark-clad occupant. "Excuse me, sir. Sorry to intrude, but we're looking for Mr. Travers. Have you seen him?" Still no answer. Was the man asleep? Perhaps he'd succumbed to the lures of brandy, a comfortable chair, and a warm fire. "Sir?"

Stepping up beside him, Phillipe tapped the man gently on the arm.

And stared as the figure tipped to one side.

Pushing back the man's hat and hood and grappling with the beak, Phillipe finally managed to yank the mask off—

—only to find Daniel Travers staring back at him, his face purpled and glittering with sweat, his mouth open, tongue swollen and protruding, eyes wide and glazed over.

The life of the party was dead.

"Bolt the doors!" Phillipe shouted to Lively, who had entered the small cabinet behind him. "No one leaves!" The officer hurried to obey. "And shut this room behind you!" The thump of the glass-paned doors gliding shut confirmed that his last order had been heard, leaving Phillipe in peace to examine the body, only Dupin with him.

There were no obvious wounds, though the dark trenchcoat could easily conceal such. Still, the flushed face and bulging eyes suggested strangulation or suffocation rather than blood loss. Nor did the air reek of spilled blood—there was only the spicy fruitiness of the brandy, the richer smoke of the fire, and a hint of something floral filling the room, as yet untainted by the stink of death.

How had he come by this second costume, though? Unfastening the straps at the collar, Phillipe pulled the coat open, revealing a black silk shirt beneath. And wadded in a pocket he found what at first looked like a black handkerchief, except for the two symmetrical holes it bore. Travers' mask. But why have two costumes at all, much less one beneath the other?

And how long had the man been sitting here, right under their noses, while they looked for him in his earlier guise?

Straightening, Phillipe sighed. Whatever had happened, this was no longer a protection detail.

It was now a murder investigation.

He heard the screams as he moved to step from the cabinet, high, anguished sounds of panic and distress. As those faded, gasps and more manly cries replaced them, startlement and concern rather than grief. Pushing through the crowd, Phillipe found them gathered around a heap of metallic color and feathers.

It seemed Miss Stevens had fainted.

Lively was there as well, and Phillipe motioned for the officer to help him lift the young lady and carry her to one of the now-vacant salons. Her mask had fallen when she did, and he scooped that up, setting it in her lap as they carried her, the pleasant scents of flowers and spice rising from their dainty burden. She stirred as they laid her down on a couch, and eyes like sapphires fluttered open, only to blink away tears.

"Oh, Daniel! Poor, poor Daniel!"

Phillipe left her to her sorrow, returning again to the dead man himself. How had he died? How had he come to be sitting there like that? And, since it seemed unlikely he had inflicted this upon himself, who had done this to him?

He was still pondering this trio of questions when someone pushed their way past the officers he'd stationed at the cabinet doors. "I will see my husband," Mrs. Travers insisted, and over her shoulder Lively shrugged helplessly. Phillipe knew it was useless to argue, and simply stepped back, allowing the fresh-made widow to reach the chair where her husband still sat.

She peered down at him, and Phillipe studied her as she did. Still an attractive woman, though a good deal older than when she had first won the famous man's attention, bitterness was written in every line and wrinkle. He saw little sign of anguish as she sniffed, nudging the body with one jewel-slippered foot.

"Well," was all she said. "Well."

Phillipe cleared his throat. "I am very sorry for your loss, ma'am," he began, and continued as she waved that off, "but perhaps you can help us determine exactly what happened?"

"What happened?" she scoffed. "Exactly what those notes said would happen. He got what was coming to him." Her eyes were glittering and hard as the diamonds she wore when she turned to him. "Did you think I'd be weeping like that little trollop out there? I knew what he was. I had more use for him alive than dead, but he *is* dead, so good riddance."

"I was surprised to find him here like this," Phillipe commented, trying a different tack. "That is not the costume he had on earlier. Nor had I seen it before."

The dead man's wife nodded. "Me either, but so what? He was always changing his mind. Throwing out the old for the new." Yes, there was that bitterness. There was something else wafting off her, however, something far more delicate, and Phillipe took a discreet sniff.

"I'm sorry, may I ask after your perfume?"

She smiled, the expression half sultry and half catty, showing a flash of the beauty she'd been in her youth. "It's called Devotion," she explained, batting her eyelashes. "Lavender, vanilla, and bergamot." Then she laughed, her smile shifting to a sneer. "He hated it. Allergic to lavender. I figured, if he's keeping his distance anyway, why not enforce it?"

But Phillipe had focused on the ingredients rather than the rationale. "Allergic, you say? Badly so?"

She nodded slowly, a sudden hint of caution to her movements. "Deathly so. I hope you're not suggesting—"

Ignoring her for the moment, he squatted to retrieve the dark mask where he'd ripped it from the victim's head. A single sniff confirmed a dizzying combination of scents and, knowing himself to be in the presence of one far more expert, Phillipe held it out for her. "Not much of a bloodhound, I'm afraid," he explained apologetically as her eyebrows rose. "Terrible sniffer."

The widow gazed askance but, after a moment, leaned in to take a ladylike whiff of the mask. "Hm, that's a potent mix, to be sure," she agreed, straightening again. "Roses, lavender, cloves, juniper, and peppermint. Ambergris as well, I think. Possibly camphor? And myrrh?" The lady shook her head, her wig wobbling with the motion. "With that up your nose, you'd never smell anything else!"

Phillipe nodded, considering the mask. "I believe that was the point. Plague doctors packed such concoctions into their masks, both to overpower the stench of bodies and because they thought it would drive away illness. But you said lavender. And your husband was allergic." He thought back to earlier. The plague doctor sitting here, twitching. Not in annoyance at being interrupted, he realized now. No, he had been witnessing a man suffering anaphylaxis, suffocating right before his eyes! Whoever the killer was, they were diabolic. And clever. And knowledgeable about Travers' weaknesses. "Who else knew about his allergy?"

Mrs. Travers tutted. "Hardly anyone, I suspect. Daniel was very concerned with appearances. Couldn't let anyone see he was weak, you know. Sharks in the water and all that." Her sneer returned. "But that's one less shark in the world, isn't it?"

She drifted away, back into the ballroom, and for a moment Phillipe considered holding her, bracing her properly. But did he really think she had killed her husband? She had motive, to be certain—jilted for a younger woman, publicly ignored, and of course she probably stood to inherit a great deal. Plus, she was wearing the same scent that had killed him. Or at least part of it. But something didn't fit.

Besides, it's not like she was going anywhere.

The where was the next question. Travers had gotten away from his guards, and wound up here, in a different costume, one that had killed him. All without anyone seeing. How?

Phillipe studied the French doors. While the party raged, someone could perhaps slip through and shut the doors behind them, but it was iffy. And why would Travers have agreed to that, anyway?

Doing a careful turn about the small room, a glint along one bookcase caught his eye. Inspecting it, Phillipe found a tiny speck, like glitter, gleaming and golden. Where had that come from? And how had it wound up here in the corner on this old, much-polished wood? Resting his hand upon the carved frame there, he started at hearing a faint click—and even more when the bookcase slid toward him, revealing a dark space behind. A hidden door!

Of course, it made sense. These little rooms were perfect for private rendezvous—but only if you could enter and exit unseen. The door led into a dark, narrow passage Phillipe saw ran all the way back behind the entire row of cabinets. Past them and the ballroom were the kitchens. One could easily slip in there and then through to any of these chambers. Plus, there might be other doors he couldn't see from here, leading out into the halls by the staterooms. He'd found his way in.

"Secret passage," Dupin croaked, and Phillipe nodded, stroking the bird's beak.

"Indeed," he agreed. "That's how Travers snuck in here. Probably still in his original costume—if he'd doffed hat and cape and sword, he'd blend in with the servers." The hat! The plague doctor hadn't been wearing one out in the ballroom, before. It was Travers' own hat, stuck atop the second costume!

So, someone had lured him in here. Then, what, overpowered him? Knocked him out? And dressed him in trenchcoat and beaked mask and hood. Sat him down, drink beside him, and snuck out the same way. Leaving the man to die a slow, horrible death with no one the wiser. Diabolical indeed, and undoubtedly a crime of passion. No one would subject Travers to such pain otherwise.

That meant whoever the original plague doctor had been, that was their killer.

And Phillipe thought he now knew who had been hiding beneath that long, pointed mask. He'd need some help to prove it, though.

"Thank you for agreeing to speak with me," he was saying a few minutes later, in another cabinet not far from the first, ill-fated one. "I hope you are recovered sufficiently?"

Miss Stevens sniffed into a lace handkerchief, the luster of her eyes only brightened by her recent tears. "Thank you," she managed, her voice quavering. "I'll do whatever I can to help, of course!" She shook her head, her blonde tresses flying. "I don't know anything, though. I didn't even see Daniel once he left for the party." She bit back a sob. "And now he's gone!"

"I'm sorry for your loss," Phillipe told her. "Yes, you had a headache earlier, is that right?" The beautiful blonde nodded. "And by the time you arrived, Mr. Travers had disappeared." He eyed her gown, that fantastical swirl of color. "It's a beautiful costume. Are those sequins?"

She nodded again, eyes demurely downcast. "Yes. Daniel picked it out for me."

"And that headpiece is magnificent," Phillipe continued. "May I?" She had not restored it atop her head, and now mutely handed it over. He examined it, even raising it to eye level before returning it to her.

"Thank you," he told her next, standing from where he'd perched on the edge of the couch she'd been draped across. "You've been very helpful." Reaching the doors, he paused and glanced back. "The only thing I don't understand," he added, "is why?"

Miss Stevens blinked up at him, a study in perplexed innocence. "Why what?"

But Phillipe was not fooled. Not anymore. "Why kill him?" he stated clearly, watching closely as the emotions ran riot across her face: shock, fear, disbelief, sorrow.

And, behind and overarching them all, rage.

But not at him.

"You came to the party with the other guests," he went on, facing her fully now. "Wearing what you have on now — with the plague doctor's coat, hood, and mask over it. Your own headpiece was stuffed into the mask — it still smells of the herbs and flowers you'd placed in there. You lured Travers into the cabinet, presumably by promising an assignation. He caused a stir to distract my officers, then slipped away, into the secret passages. You were waiting for him. Did you drug him? Or just cut off his air supply? You slipped off your disguise and put it on him instead, making sure to fit the mask tightly over his face. You knew about his allergy, of course. Then you exited through the bookcase—I found one of your sequins caught on it—to make your triumphant appearance at the main doors. Thus, you were well away from him, and out in the open, when he was found dead." He shook his head. "Very clever, really. I just don't know why."

"Why?" Her beautiful face twisted in fury. "He was a vulture! A shark! He stripped people of their lives, their money, their dignity, all to make himself fatter! He ruined everyone he touched—just like the real plague doctors, taking people's last coins and promising them cures but delivering only death! People like my father, who owned a small shop in a building Daniel wanted to tear down and replace. So he ruined Papa, drove him to drink and despair and death, laughing all the while." She lifted her chin, proud and undaunted and a thousand times more stunning for it. "Well, it took me years, but I'm the one laughing now!"

"Laughing death," Dupin cawed as if agreeing. The crow was still fluttering its wings as Phillipe exited the room, closing the door gently behind him. Miss Stevens wasn't going anywhere, and she clearly wasn't concerned about trying to escape or about hiding what she'd done. It must have been terrible, pretending affection for Travers all this time, just to get close enough to do him in. And now she had.

Was it worth it? Phillipe wondered. Did she feel unburdened now that her father's killer had been killed in turn?

Though the *Prospero* was lighter than air, he felt a heavy tug as he turned away, leaving the lovely murderess to her thoughts and her solitude.

They would all return to earth soon enough.

Dreams of Flight

David Lee Summers

PROFESSOR M.K. MARAVILLA BENT OVER A BLACK, feathered form about two feet long. Illumination came from a hole in the roof of the abandoned cabin he now occupied, which he suspected once belonged to one of the lumbermen who traded in the settlement some seventy-five miles away. He peered inside the raven's body through jeweler's loops attached to a pair of magnifying glasses, accessing the final assemblage of tiny springs, cogs, and gears gathered over months of travel for the sole purpose of collecting cast-off watches, metronomes, music boxes, and compasses—anything with parts he might use in his experiments. He made one careful adjustment with his tiny screwdriver, then examined his work. He assured the wax cylinder for recording bird calls and other natural sounds would rotate unimpeded. He checked the tension of the springs. Just one more thing to do.

He reached for a heart-shaped locket that once belonged to his daughter, Verdad. Inside lay a lock of her raven hair. He touched it with longing. Together they had dreamed of her becoming a scientist and engineer like him. Birds and flight fascinated her. They had loved studying them together. Those dreams had died, as had she. He closed the locket and kissed it before nestling it in the bird's chest compartment. His task complete, Maravilla carefully fastened the hatch lest he disturb the inner clockworks. He sat back, removed the magnifying lenses, and admired his work.

He'd found the raven's body at a trading post in the settlement called Flagstaff, where lumberjacks took their logs to the trains passing through Northern Arizona. One of the clerks at the post also practiced taxidermy. He'd done fine work preserving the bird. Maravilla had hated cutting the fine stitches and removing the sawdust and stiff wire framework, but he was on a mission. Now, to see if his project had succeeded. He cradled the raven—filled with clockworks, springs, gears, and a lightweight framework connected with hinges and ball socket joints—and took it outside, where he gasped at the view before him, a visage at once frightening, sublime, and glorious.

An enormous rift cleaved the earth as far as he could see, both east and west. The sight frightened him with its profound depths. He found it magnificent in its strange gigantic forms and glorious in its colors. Bold striations of red, yellow, white, and greenish-gray striped the great rift's walls. Here and there, he glimpsed the river almost a mile below him. He stood on the rim of the Grand Canyon, which thrilled him with its witchery of light and shade.

Verdad would have loved this place.

He closed his eyes at the memory of her screams as soldiers took her and her mother away from him. They had shot his wife and daughter to punish him for his loyalty to Mexico's previous regime. He thought French rule had brought a civilizing influence to the New World, and he'd supported Napoleon III. The Mexican revolutionaries who'd invaded his home stripped the veneer of civilization away in a heartbeat. His family's final screams still echoing in his head, Maravilla had broken free from the soldiers who'd held him captive and fled in a hail of bullets. He eventually escaped his native Mexico and settled in Northern Arizona. The solitude of this wild place allowed him to continue his studies of the natural world, including his desire to understand how birds fly… a desire prompted by his daughter's innocent questions.

He turned the raven over and wound a tiny hidden key, then stood the raven on its feet. It hopped twice and tilted its head. A living raven flew down from a nearby tree and mimicked the simulacrum. Maravilla laughed and clapped his hands in delight as dark memories faded. Startled, the living raven flew to the cabin's roof.

The clockwork raven hopped twice more, then spread its wings. It gave a mighty flap, then took to the air, flew two circles just as it had been designed to, and landed on the ground. Maravilla watched, mesmerized, as the raven repeated the pattern a second time, then crashed into a tree on its final circle. The professor ran over and retrieved his creation, dusted it off, and breathed a relieved sigh when he could find no damage. He returned it to the ground, satisfied with his experiment. It had moved quite splendidly and almost naturally, if a bit stiff and predictable, as though its life had been extended. He thought this raven should have a name. Although Verdad seemed appropriate, the reminder would be too painful.

He remembered a tale… "The Facts in the Case of M. Valdemar," written by a fancier of ravens about a man whose life had been extended through the power of mesmerism. He murmured the name aloud: "Valdemar." It even started with a "V." Close, but not too close to his daughter's name. He smiled at his creation. "I think that would be a splendid name for you, my friend: The Great Winged Valdemar, or simply Valdemar for short."

Maravilla wound the flight clockworks again. The mechanical raven repeated its routine three times before winding down, this time without hitting any trees. The living raven on the cabin's roof flew down and studied the clockwork creation for a moment. It squawked at the mechanical raven as if in encouragement. Maravilla nodded to himself. If Valdemar recorded enough sounds, he could reset the cylinder inside, and his clockwork creation would caw like a real raven.

Professor Maravilla went inside the cabin and left the living raven and Valdemar to interact. He hoped he might get more natural bird noises if he wasn't present. The professor may have fallen on hard times, but he endeavored to maintain his dignity and bearing. He discarded his apron, then donned a clean shirt and short coat. As he dressed, the sound of chattering ravens increased outside.

He left the cabin and looked around. Ravens filled every tree surrounding his clearing. They all squawked and chattered as though having an animated discussion. They bobbed and swooped down, only to wing up again. As for Valdemar, it stood poised as before, as if to take flight, only more natural this time, the body and legs slightly tensed to propel it upward. For a moment, he wondered if the clockworks simply hadn't run down as he'd assumed. The clockwork raven turned its head back, looking for all the world as if it checked to ensure Maravilla watched. The ebony eye twinkled as it had not the first time before the bird turned back forward, flapped its mighty wings, and took flight, coming to land among the other corvids, its heavier body dipping the branch. He couldn't explain a flight from the ground to a tree branch.

As he watched in awe, Maravilla remembered the tales told by the Pueblo tribes in the neighboring territory, legends of a powerful godlike being—a Kachina—called Crow Mother. She initiated young people into Pueblo religious life. Raised Catholic, Maravilla could never shake the idea that the world held deeper mysteries than those easily observed through science. Could it be that Crow Mother had sent her children to initiate Valdemar into the ways of being a raven? The idea intrigued him. How else to explain this transformation…

As if rather pleased to have shown off its new skill, Valdemar cocked its head toward him, then flew down to light on his shoulder.

With a cacophony of raucous caws, the other ravens flew off along the canyon's rim.

Maravilla barely noticed, gripped by an intense urge to take the clockwork back inside to examine it in detail. Valdemar's head, however, darted forward toward the retreating ravens. The inventor frowned. The mechanical raven shouldn't be able to do that.

Valdemar gently, if insistently, tapped Maravilla's head with its… his beak and again pointed in the direction the ravens had flown.

"Hmph. Fine, then, I guess you want me to see what's over there." Maravilla followed the trail a short distance. A frown tugged gently at his lips as he noticed smoke from a point that jutted into the canyon about two miles away. It was still early in the summer. The monsoon rains had not started, and there had been no lightning to spark the underbrush. The fire must be manmade. His pace quickened. Fire and other humans may be necessities, but both could pose a danger in his experience.

He glanced at Valdemar on his shoulder. He couldn't shake the thought the ravens had adopted the mechanical corvid as a brother and somehow told him about the distant fire. Ravens, in general, seemed to have enough intelligence for him to believe that much, but Valdemar should not be able to take independent action. He plucked the clockwork corvid from his shoulder and wound his key but disengaged the clutch that enabled flight before settling the raven back on his perch.

Returning to his cabin, Maravilla grabbed a bowler and spyglass, then set out to determine the smoke's source. He followed a deer trail near the canyon's rim but kept close to the trees, periodically examining the distant terrain with his spyglass. At last, he reached a point where he could make out the source of the smoke.

Ahead, some three dozen men erected large tents and unloaded wagonloads of equipment while others tended the horses and mules. As he continued his walk, the camp's hubbub reached the professor's ears. Someone tended a cookfire, the savory aroma of beans and bacon enticing, but the scent of scorched coffee less so.

This was no military expedition. None of them wore uniforms, not even those who appeared to be in charge. By the same token, this group was too large and well-equipped — not to mention organized — to be an outlaw band hiding out. He continued forward with caution but lessened concern.

As he crept closer, more of their equipment came into view. On a table sat barometers, which could be used for determining elevation, and sextants, for determining latitude and longitude, along with a clinometer similar to the one employed by Darwin himself to triangulate location and height in the field. Maravilla also noticed rock hammers and several cases holding blowpipes, and some of the men wore hand lenses around their necks. One box set ever so gently on a central table must have held the team's precious microscope. Maravilla relaxed even more. These were clearly geologists and fellow scientists.

Moving with less stealth but just as much care, he entered the camp, raising his hands in the air as he went. The first two men to notice him immediately drew revolvers. A wave of muttering moved through the camp as all activity ceased.

Maravilla stopped where he stood, arms still raised, body as relaxed as he could manage, staring down two blued barrels, a horrible echo of that time before. "I'm all alone. I mean you no ill will. I was in the area and curious about your investigations."

A gray-haired man emerged from the largest tent. "I'm Dr. George Bain, leader of this expedition." Notably, the man did not order his men to lower their weapons.

"I'm Professor M.K. Maravilla, an engineer interested in the mechanics of flight. I'm in the area because I can watch ravens, condors, and hawks fly long distances."

Bain lifted his chin. "Is that raven on your shoulder a trained bird? I've never seen one sit so still."

"Not exactly. I still have much to learn about this creature." Maravilla's eyes shifted to Valdemar. He wanted to know about these geologists before he revealed more about his creation. "Tell me what you hope to learn from your expedition."

"We're here to explore the canyon for mineral wealth," Bain said.

As he spoke, a woman wearing a man's shirt and trousers emerged from the large tent looking enough like Dr. Bain to surely be his daughter. The sight of her made Maravilla gasp. What might Verdad have looked like if she'd been allowed to grow a little older?

The woman looked from Bain to the men with the revolvers.

"Percy, Clarence, lower your weapons." She approached Maravilla. "I'm Delitha Bain. Why don't you come sit down, and we'll talk." She laid a hand on his arm and led Maravilla past the tent to a place where a camp table and chairs had been set up.

After helping her to sit, Maravilla moved the heavy mechanical raven to the table. "What brings a young woman like you to a remote place like this?"

Delitha looked to Bain. "My father is a mining engineer. I hope to join him in the profession. Preliminary surveys by teams such as Major Powell's a few years ago suggest great mineral wealth here in the Grand Canyon."

As she spoke of her aspirations, Maravilla was again reminded of his daughter. Unlike Verdad, Delitha had blue eyes and light brown hair, but their build and demeanor were similar. He delighted in the sparkle of intelligence in her gaze, something else both of them shared.

Maravilla sighed. "I have only met one other young lady who aspired to be an engineer." His voice caught as he spoke of his late daughter. "Her dreams came to an abrupt end."

Delitha nodded. "I'm sorry to hear that. U.C. Berkeley just granted a woman an engineering degree. I'm looking for a way to convince a university to admit me." She spoke without understanding the depths of Maravilla's loss, only to trail off as she noticed her father standing over them, arms crossed in front of his chest, eyeing the professor suspiciously. Maravilla knew Bain didn't trust him. He didn't know whether the lack of trust came because he was a stranger or because he was Mexican.

"Father, please get us some coffee, then sit down and join us instead of standing there glowering."

Bain softened a bit at his daughter's gentle gibe. Moving to a trivet over a nearby fire, he retrieved a tin percolator and three metal mugs, blue with white speckles. He passed them around and poured the coffee before sitting down. "Are you familiar with geology, Professor… what was your name again?"

"Maravilla. I took classes on the way to my degree, but I'm no expert. My interest is in mechanical devices. I hope to find a way to make a machine fly."

Bain laughed outright, but Delitha sat forward, her gaze going wide a moment before narrowing as she looked from Maravilla to Valdemar. "Your raven, he's not just well-behaved. He's clockwork, is he not?"

Maravilla beamed. "He is. May I present the Great Winged Valdemar?" He moved the clockwork raven to the ground and released his clutch. Valdemar hopped twice, then gave his wings a strong flap and another before taking flight and making three circles as he had been designed to do, as though Valdemar knew enough not to reveal too many newfound talents. Both Bain and his daughter caught their breath.

"That is a remarkable toy," Delitha whispered.

"I hope, in the long run, to build more than a toy." When Valdemar landed, Maravilla engaged his clutch and set him back on the table. "I hope to build a machine big enough to allow a person to fly through the air and see the world as a bird does."

Delitha and her father exchanged glances. George Bain stood and put his hand on Maravilla's shoulder, then pointed toward the Grand Canyon. "I fully expect that we will stake a claim somewhere in the great expanse before us. Despite my confidence, the biggest challenge will be getting that mineral wealth out of a mile-deep hole in the ground. A flying machine could be invaluable to such an aim."

Maravilla's brow furrowed as he noticed Delitha eyeing Valdemar. Verdad would have eyed the mechanical raven with wonder. Delitha wore a sly grin.

"Such an aim would require a device that could carry the weight of both a human and the ore you hope to mine."

Bain shrugged. "Your machine is quite good at independent flight. It could be sent from the mine to the rim all by itself." The geological engineer turned to face Maravilla. "Would you be willing to sell us the plans to your mechanical raven? I'd be prepared to pay a large sum."

Maravilla grasped the raven protectively. "I'm afraid that would be impossible."

Delitha raised her hands to her chest. "I don't understand. Surely, you don't think we would try to cheat you out of credit for your invention." The professor thought her shock a little too exaggerated to be real.

Maravilla shook his head. "It's not that. There are no plans." He tapped his head. "Or rather, the plans are all up here. People have stolen from me before. Also, I have learned that sometimes I do my best work based on inspiration. I don't draft plans ahead of time. I improvise and make improvements as I go. I figure out what works and what doesn't. Once I have a working model, and I'm satisfied it does everything I want, I can then, very carefully, take it apart and make drawings."

Bain leaned forward, a little too eagerly for the professor's taste. "We would pay handsomely for those drawings."

Maravilla frowned as he caught sight of the two guards who had aimed weapons at him a short time before. "I'm not sure I'm satisfied with Valdemar yet. I don't know how robust his clockworks are, and even then, I'm not sure I want to sell the plans. Selling my designs to you may prevent me from continuing my work."

Delitha sat forward and put her hand on Maravilla's. "We wouldn't dream of preventing you from using your designs for scientific research. We would only want them for the commercial application."

Maravilla gazed into Delitha's blue eyes, which seemed somehow colder than they had moments before. Her small mouth curled into a frown, and her lower lip threatened to protrude in a pout. A part of him wanted to grant this young woman her wish. Still, something twisted in his gut. He knew she manipulated him. She had her own objectives. He could negotiate and possibly benefit from an arrangement with these people, but he needed time to think and determine the best course of action. He also needed more information about them and thought he knew how to get it.

"You must understand, I did not build Valdemar… the raven… for personal profit. I built him for research. I might be willing to work with you, but I need time to consider appropriate terms."

"Of course," Bain said, his words clipped. "Take all the time you need."

Maravilla stood. Transferring Valdemar to his shoulder, he shook hands with Bain and briefly clasped Delitha's hand before turning and walking away from the mining engineers' camp, tipping his hat to the guards, Clarence and Percy. He meandered through the trees a short distance, not following any particular trail. He stood for a time, thinking of the exchange.

Setting Valdemar on a low branch, he flipped a hidden lever near the raven's key. Then, looking deep into the black bead eyes, he murmured, "Go… go listen, but don't let them see you." He then held his breath, praying whatever had transformed his creation had gifted it with a raven's intelligence as well.

The mechanical raven bobbed his head as if in answer before crouching on the branch and launching into the air. Maravilla watched as he flew back toward the engineer's camp before proceeding to his lonely cabin.

The professor reached his home a little after noon. After checking on his horses to make sure they were happy and healthy, he took some time to neaten up around the cabin and his workbench. His chores done, the professor prepared to venture out to retrieve his creation, only to startle as Valdemar alighted on the cabin's windowsill.

"How did you find your way back here?" he murmured before he remembered the ravens in the trees earlier, chattering while Valdemar appeared to listen. Again, he remembered Crow Mother, who initiated the young, leading them to adulthood, to independence.

Before he could lift the raven from the windowsill, a rough pair of hands snatched the mechanical bird.

"Gotcha!"

Maravilla recognized the voice of Bain's guard, Percy.

The professor ran to the door in time to see the man handing off the bird to his mounted partner, Clarence, before clambering onto his horse.

"Damn bird just crapped like the real thing. Realism can go too far," complained the thief as they rode away.

Maravilla rushed to where they'd mounted their horses. There, among the pine needles, he found a small wax cylinder smaller than a spool of thread. How? How had Valdemar ejected the cylinder? Maravilla would never know, but he thanked the divine that the bird had. He picked up the recording cylinder and took it into the cabin. He placed it on a rotating arm, wound it up, then placed a needle into grooves on the wax. First, he heard his own voice, then, for about five minutes, nothing but forest sounds intermixed with the caws of ravens. Finally, he heard voices.

"If I could get the mechanical raven, I could take it apart and make the plans myself," Delitha Bain said, the sound a little flat and tinny. *"It wouldn't even have to carry a large payload to bring me to the attention of a good engineering school."*

"And if we could re-engineer it to carry minerals, it would solve many of our problems," her father agreed.

Maravilla frowned, more disappointed than angry that his worst suspicions had been confirmed. He continued to listen.

"We can't bring it back here. This is the first place he'll look," Delitha said.

"I'll have Percy and Clarence nab it and meet you in Flagstaff. You can get a room at the Weatherford and take all the time you need."

Maravilla rubbed the bridge of his nose. He could try tailing Percy and Clarence, but he was no tracker. Flagstaff was a good three-day ride if he didn't push his horse too hard. He knew a good route and might be able to shave off a few hours. He stopped the cylinder, packed food for a week, and went out to saddle his best horse.

Professor Maravilla rode as hard and fast as he could through the wooded countryside without exhausting his horse. Along the way, he noted many ravens in the trees, seemingly urging him on to save their brother, even guiding him—he dare say—along quicker paths.

He reached Flagstaff in the middle of the third day. Despite the urgency driving him, he could not help but note the changes since his last visit, impressed with how the settlement began to resemble a town. Even so, he traveled down familiar streets. Passing the lumber mill and the trading post, he headed toward the railroad station. As he neared, he waved to the local blacksmith, Leroy Foster, who strolled down the street chatting with a sharp-eyed, silver-haired woman who called herself Lady Junesquirrel.

The blacksmith waved back.

"Good to see you, professor," the woman said. The professor doubted the American woman had been granted a peerage or that "Junesquirrel" was her real name, but she had supported his work and, given his history, the professor understood there were many reasons why one might adopt a new sobriquet.

Maravilla tugged on his reins, slowing the horse to a walk, keeping pace with his friends. "How are things?"

Foster ran his fingers through shortened hair. "A barber just set up shop a little over a week ago. He wanted to pull one of my teeth, but I drew the line at cutting my hair."

"A good thing, too. I would barely trust that man with scissors much less pliers," the woman said.

Maravilla chuckled despite his worry. *Once all of this is settled, a haircut might be welcome,* he thought as they reached the settlement's lone hotel, the Weatherford, which sat across from the railroad station. Maravilla dismounted and tied his horse to the hitching post.

"What brings you to town?" Lady Junesquirrel asked, coming to a stop with him and Foster.

"Some geologists took one of my inventions. I'm pretty sure they came here."

"Need some help persuading these *geologists* to give it back?" The blacksmith rubbed his hands as though itching for a good brawl. The woman looked ready to help him.

Perhaps it was Delitha's resemblance to his daughter, or perhaps it was again losing something precious to him at the hands of armed men, but dark memories he'd at one time been good at burying again came to the surface. Memories of soldiers bursting into his house… taking his wife… taking Verdad. Maravilla shuddered. Miss Bain may have angered him, but she didn't deserve violence. Still, his friends' support heartened him. "Let me try talking to them first. If I need help, I'll let you know."

"You know where to find me." Foster pointed up the road to his shop, and Lady Junesquirrel flashed a reassuring smile.

Maravilla tipped his hat and entered the Weatherford.

"Ah, professor, what brings you into town?" The hotel clerk—a Navajo named Chee—greeted him.

"Did a woman check in? Her name is Delitha Bain." He doubted she'd hide her identity, but he described her just in case. "She likely would have worn men's clothes."

The clerk chuckled. "A lot of women around here do. But yes, Miss Bain and two gentlemen checked in about fifteen minutes ago. I'll take you up to her room."

Maravilla's heart leapt in his chest as the clerk led him upstairs. He prayed he wasn't too late. As they approached the room, something thumped, followed by a woman's pained squeal and the sound of fluttering.

The clerk knocked with some urgency on the door. "Miss Bain? Miss Bain, is everything okay?" After a moment of long, sudden silence, he persisted. "Miss Bain, I must insist you open the door."

Delitha's muffled growl betrayed her annoyance. There was the scuffing of furniture, and then a moment later, she opened the door, a tendril of blood dripping from a scratch on her temple and her hair mussed. A scowl twisted her expression, deepening at the sight of Maravilla. "Didn't take you long to find me. I thought you'd waste more time returning to our camp."

"I had help. You haven't tried to open Valdemar, have you?"

"I just arrived. But as soon as I set to work, the damn bird flew up into the rafters. I haven't been able to get it down." Delitha stepped back and allowed Maravilla and the clerk to enter a nice, airy room with a tall ceiling. Valdemar perched on a rafter above the bed. From the state of the blankets, Delitha must have been trying to jump high enough on the bed to grab the rafter or the mechanical bird.

"If you'll allow me to assist?" Maravilla said.

The words scarcely left his mouth when someone seized him and the clerk from behind. Maravilla frowned and shook his head, whether in disappointment at himself or disgust at the perfidy of this woman, he found it difficult to say. How could he have forgotten the men with her?

"Not a chance, pal. This bird is my one opportunity. If you do indeed have the plans stored in your noggin," Delitha pointed to Maravilla's head, "then you can surely build another for yourself. This one's mine now. I strongly suggest you leave of your own accord. Percy and Clarence are quite capable… *chaperones*. If you force the issue, they will see you out by the most expedient means possible."

Percy began to tug Maravilla toward the door while Delithia turned away, moving to lift a large basin as if to bring the bird down by more violent means. Maravilla gasped and started to resist, not wishing his creation to be damaged, even if it meant sacrificing the raven to these thieves to ensure he survived.

"Please, allow me to bring Valdemar down from the rafters."

Delitha frowned, then looked from the bird to the bed and nodded. "All right, but any funny business and Percy will eliminate you."

Percy released the professor and drew his sidearm. Maravilla did his best to ignore the weapon as he climbed up on the bed. Valdemar took two steps away of his own volition. The professor knew that shouldn't be possible. Still, he considered what he'd seen—Valdemar in the trees listening to the ravens, Valdemar leading him to the geologists' camp, Valdemar returning to his cabin on his own.

Maravilla held up his arm and clucked his tongue. Valdemar bobbed his head, then flew onto the offered forearm.

Holding onto the headboard, Maravilla stepped off the bed and carried him to a vanity, where the bird hopped off.

"What kind of springs did you use in that bird? I can't believe it's still flying and moving after three days." Delitha's scientific curiosity seemed to override her greed for a moment. The professor thought there might be hope for her yet. "It almost seems to make decisions on its own." She held her hand to the scratch on her temple.

"I don't know," Maravilla admitted. "I assembled the springs, gears, cogs, and armatures that serve as muscles for this poor creature, but even I do not fully understand Valdemar's independence. It is… a miracle."

"Ravens are creatures of transition," the hotel clerk said. "Childhood to adulthood. Life to death."

"Life is a mystery," Maravilla said. "A mystery far greater than any scientific achievement of man, I suspect." He reached toward Valdemar. The mechanical raven hopped backward toward the vanity's mirror.

"Nevermore," Valdemar gasped, even though he had no means to speak without the wax cylinder. As he said that, first one feather fell, then another. A moment later, the raven's chest panel opened, and the heart-shaped locket fell out. Maravilla picked it up, somehow knowing it was a parting gift.

Valdemar's wing dropped off, then one of his legs. It toppled over on its side. No life remained in its glass eyes. Maravilla suspected he held the raven's spirit in his hand.

"What have you done?" Delitha pushed him aside and grabbed the bird. As she did, springs flew out of the raven's chest compartment. Within, gears, cogs, and pistons sat willy-nilly as though assorted clockworks and mechanisms had simply been placed within a raven's carcass with no rhyme or reason.

Like Poe's M. Valdemar, the mechanical raven's life had come to a terrible end, and nothing could be done to revive it again.

Professor Maravilla sighed and removed his hat. "The world is not a fair place, Miss Bain. Your father's enterprise will give you many opportunities to show your capabilities as an engineer, and I wish you success. I will continue my research, but please do not attempt to steal from me again. There shall not be another Valdemar."

The professor placed his hat on his head and Verdad's locket in his pocket next to his heart before turning his back on the woman forever more.

Unimpeded, he left the room.

CROWBAIT

JUDI FLEMING

EDGAR ALLAN CROW PAUSED IN HIS FLIGHT UP TO THE tower. He alighted on the gas streetlamp's elegant arched iron curl and wished he could smooth and clean his feathers before approaching his food giver with his latest find. The clever young human had morsels tasty enough to brave the raven and her food giver in the same noisy tower room, yet the prize in his beak kept him from straightening feathers made rough and unruly by the chugging machines clamoring and chuffing steam on the street below him.

Crow liked the horses better. Their humans never minded Crow filching the grain the horses spilled from their lunchtime nosebags. He just had to be careful of the noisy machines puffing by with their popinjay riders in colorful cloth coverings and bright, bright, ever-so-tempting buttons across their fronts. Crow flitted to the top of the tower on the building in front of him, listening carefully to movements inside before hopping down to the open window.

"Crow!" his human shouted, "What have you got for me today?"

The morsels of bread and cheese were eagerly exchanged for the shiny trinket, and he cawed his delight over the trade. It was hard for him to eat and look at all the shiny bits and bobs arranged across the desktop he had perched upon to collect his bounty.

"Oh, a pocket watch. Clever, clever Crow. I should have all the parts I need now for my invention."

Crow greedily gulped the last bit of stale bread down his gullet and peered at the small human, noting the soothing brown shades of his clothing, thick black curls of hair, and bare, clawless feet. He admired his clever little human and cawed loudly again, asking for more food.

"Sorry, Crow, that's all I can spare right now. Master might catch me if I pinch any more than I already do. He's mean, that one is." The boy rubbed his bruise-blackened cheek as he spoke.

A *clunk* downstairs made the boy jump and whirl around to face the open door of the curious, trinket-filled room.

"Tomas!" the deep voice boomed as the stairs thudded under the ponderous weight of the large human Crow had learned to be wary of. "Tomas, where the bloody hell are you, boy?"

A huge raven swirled into the room, slamming a sharp beak on the boy's head as it arrowed toward Crow, its much hoarser and deeper caws echoing in the tall-ceilinged room.

Crow squawked and tumbled down and out of the window, turning his lighter body mid-flap up and around to the top of the towered roof, ducking behind the circular slate roof before the raven could catch sight of his slight-of-wing disappearing act.

Inside, Tomas quaked in fear as his master thundered into the room, his own sleight-of-hand movements covering the fact that he pocketed the watch Crow had gifted him.

"Sir?" he croaked, sounding more like his crow than he had intended. His head smarted from that wicked raven's beak. Damned bird did that every single time.

His master stripped off his bright red coat to reveal his white silk shirt like an apple being peeled of its skin. He tossed his top hat, goggles, and coat directly at Tomas' face even as he loosened his green satin ascot and barked, "I need the toolboxes F and G, and bring me the smallest of small oil cans with the fine tips. I have a new commission, and we must hurry to finish quickly to get the bonus for having it done by midnight." As the raven settled onto the marble bust at the corner of the table, the man stroked its head. "And fetch me the address from my calendar."

"Yes, sir, right away, sir," Tomas dashed from the room, carefully hanging his master's items, checking the appointment book, and writing out the address before running back to the workroom. He gently pulled the three carefully labeled boxes from their organized cubbies that took up the greater portion of the south wall. When he turned back, his master had struggled out of his brilliantly hued vest and was rummaging around the worktop, selecting pieces of half-made machines or odd gears and pins. Tomas winced at the destruction of his careful organization as he thought of the hours of work it would take to put it right again to avoid another beating. Still, he placed the boxes on the worktable within easy reach and silently stepped back next to the master's shoulder, ready for the next request and to watch and learn. Always watch and learn.

After three hours of steady work, Tomas gasped aloud and instantly covered his mouth with his hand, trying to choke back the involuntary reaction.

His master turned slowly, flipping the lens of the delicately stacked spectacle levers away from his right eye with greater care than what such large fingers should have allowed. The clockwork items in the room seemed louder in the sudden chill silence between them. "You have something to say, my young scoundrel?" he asked. The raven squawked a harsh laugh.

"N-n-no, sir. My apologies, sir." Tomas cringed, looking to the floor.

"You seem to have forgotten one of the most basic rules of my household. You are here to serve my every whim, speak only when spoken to, and never, ever interrupt my work."

"Yes, sir. So very sorry, sir. It won't happen again." But Tomas knew it was already too late. The red crept up from the fat man's neck, blossoming across his round cheeks as he worked himself into a rage.

"I take you off the streets. Provide you food, clothing, and shelter, and I ask so very little of you in return."

"Return," echoed his raven.

The man stood, and Tomas tried not to cower backward as his master cuffed him hard across his already bruised cheek. "I shall discipline you properly after I have bathed and washed the signs of my labor from myself and deliver this delicate automaton to Sir Alfred's party tonight. Go, draw the bath and set out my clothing, and we shall ensure that you nevermore waste my valuable time."

Again, his cold words were interrupted by the raven, who squawked, "Nevermore."

Tomas flew instantly into motion, dashing out of the room to do all his master commanded.

When all was perfectly done, and his master had gone off, raven clucking like a clock on his shoulder, after having locked the many and varied and impossible locks on the door that held Tomas captive in this great house, Tomas carefully cupped his cheek and let out another soft sigh. He thought of the clever expanding box his master had made, recalling how the gears turned and unfolded each perfectly couched layers of thin metal one after the next to reveal the mirrored surface of what could only be a place to hold a ring. Such beautiful artistry from such a vicious man only reinforced Tomas' belief in the cruelty of his lot to be a low-born and orphaned in such society. Where every technological wonder was revealed to him by a man who would never allow him to create such beautiful machines himself. To always be stuck in his role as servant with no say in his own destiny. All because he had tried picking the wrong pocket when this man crossed his path nearly two years ago.

He cleaned the workroom quickly and efficiently before setting the new pocket watch on the table. His nimble fingers stripped the case and teased apart the tiny gears and spring, laying each out carefully before ducking under the heavy table to pull his own creation from within a cleverly disguised cubby secreted beneath the worktable where his master's bulk would make it difficult for him to search. Tomas thought a word of thanks to Crow, his only friend, for bringing him precisely what he had needed. He held the small automaton in the palm of his hand where its tiny legs and body scarcely covered his palm. Selecting each of the final pieces he needed for the clockwork, he bent to his task of finishing his masterpiece before the master returned.

The routine of the morning did nothing to soothe Tomas' nerves as he listened attentively to his master's snores and the raven's sleepy grumbling in the darkened bedroom above the dining room as he prepared the breakfast. He carefully slipped tiny portions into his pocket, knowing Crow would come later after the Master went out to the salons in the afternoon. Once he had punished Tomas. A cold shiver ran down his spine as he set out the plates, ever so careful to make no noise as he set each down as quietly as a down feather falling on the rich linen tablecloth.

He thought of his secret machine stashed upstairs and waiting as he crept up the stairs to sit on the hard stool outside the bedroom and await his master's waking.

Some hours later, the man was clean, dressed, and fed, with Tomas standing silently at his station, awaiting to be called forth. The rings on the man's fingers sparked as he tapped his steepled fingertips together.

"What to do. What to do," he said while staring off into the distance. The raven echoed "Do! Do! Do!" in its mocking laughter, turning its head, so that first one and then the other liquid black eye focused on him. Outside, the echoing caws of crows sounded in the distance.

Tomans was quieter than a mouse, knowing after long experience that he shouldn't speak or even twitch. His heart raced, and his palms sweat as he forced himself to stand impassively.

"Well, I have to say I've become accustomed to being better served these past two years. So, tossing you out like yesterday's rubbish is quite distasteful. After all, your penance for thieving still must be realized." The master tapped his straining vest pocket, which contained his wallet. The great folds of flesh at the man's chin quivered as he barked out an unexpected laugh. "I fancy that I've invested a great deal of my valuable time training you to serve me properly. Me, the most accomplished artificer in the city. It's almost as if you understood my workings, anticipating my tools. You should be humbled by such an opportunity, and yet you persist in interrupting my work. No, booting you out will not do."

Tomas felt a bead of sweat trickle down the center of his back as he held his breath, a faint kernel of hope igniting like a gas lamp in his chest. He had grown used to eating, if not the beatings. The cawing of crows grew closer.

The master pulled the chain of a magnificent pocket watch, drawing it out and clicking it open to check the time. The raven leaned over his shoulder, peering closely at the shiny bauble, and the man stroked the bird's chin as if it were a cat.

"I shall have to ponder this further. My appointment with my next client approaches." He heaved his bulk up from the table, the elegant china clinked as the chair scraped back. "Clean the windows today. All of them. Even the ones in the attic and basement."

"Yes, sir," Tomas replied instantly. Not a word more or less than he was expected to say. He helped the man into his great waistcoat, ducking a sharp peck from the raven as he buttoned the golden buttons, then he rushed to the door to await with the master's smart hat and cane, only breathing a sigh of relief as the last key withdrew from the series of locks that graced the front door, just like all the others and each window of his prison.

The hoarse "caw, caw, caw" of Crow was already upstairs, having arrived in the only open window, too high above the busy street with no handholds down to the freedom of the city. The raven, after all, was granted his liberty any time he wished.

Tomas quickly plunked the remaining boiled eggs into his pocket with the other morsels he had divided up between himself and his friend, stuffing his portion in his mouth from the master's leavings as he cleared the dishes. He dashed up the stairs and into the workroom to spy Crow standing on the windowsill, eyeing the glittering gears arranged in neat piles on the master's workshop.

"Leave them, Crow. I'll not take a beating for your love of shiny things. Take these eggs instead, and let me get the rest of our breakfast out so we can eat properly." Tomas followed words with actions and laid out the food.

Crow became very eager and danced across the tabletop lightly, wings spread as he created enough lift to barely touch the surface with his clawed feet.

"Stop it before you spill the containers of parts, Crow!" he nearly shouted but followed it with a happy laugh to see such antics. The crow tried to pick up a boiled egg, but it rolled unsteadily toward the back edge of the workbench and into the dark space behind, hitting the floor with a thump.

Crow cawed angrily. A perfectly good egg would not get the better of him. He arrowed his body into the space, grumbling to himself in a coarse, throaty voice that almost sounded like a steam engine starting up. The egg had properly cracked open, and he gulped pieces down, shells and all. The front door slammed open, and he froze in place. Never before had the raven's food giver come back to the dwelling this early in the morning. He scuttled into the shadows afforded by the heavy drapes around the window behind the workbench and held himself very still.

He could hear his human hastily cleaning the workbench of all those delicious things, and the heavy beating of wings as the raven soared into the room. His human gasped in pain as the larger man's footsteps made the stairs creak as he trudged up. Crow could hear the raven's claws tapping on the workbench and hear his greedy mumbling as he ate the leftover crumbs above his head, the steady tapping of his beak as he plucked up the food that should belong to crow making him angry.

"Oh, good you are up here, Tomas. Fetch me my toolkit and the two simply clockwork birds. Lady Josephine would like to see some examples of such work." The man paused, looking at the workbench, and he scowled. "Have you been eating on my workbench, young sir?" Even as he said it, his face flushed, and his meaty hands clenched into a fist.

"No, sir!" Tomas stammered as he turned away from the table, heading toward the doorway as if he could flee. Nowhere was a safe hiding place in his master's house. Not with all the geared gadgets that could creep into corners and behind all the curtains and clamor in alarm, bringing the fat man and his wrath down upon him.

"You ungrateful, churlish boy. I have simple rules in my house, and you seem to flaunt them more and more often." He raised a fist, and Tomas stepped back to the stairwell, raising his own hands as if he could defend himself against the much larger man.

He could see the swing coming and ducked. The forward momentum of the man's swing overbalanced him when he failed to strike flesh, and he tumbled forward, slamming and bouncing hard enough that at least one stair tread crunched and broke as the heavy body plunged downward.

The raven screeched and flew down the stair, circled, and came back up, fury plain in its guttural caws. It reached its talons out and raked Tomas' face, and he cried out in pain, alternating between covering his face and batting the huge black bird away from his eyes.

Crow saw it all very clearly from his vantage under the table. First, Raven had eaten his food, and now he attacked his food giver. If Crow didn't act quickly, he knew the evil bird would peck out his eyes. He puffed his feathers and launched himself, spiraling up and out from under the workbench, striking the larger bird as hard as he could. And black feathers flew. The raven struck the wood floor, and his human grabbed it almost without thinking and flung it hard against the wall, where it lay crumpled and unmoving.

Both breathed heavily as they tried to listen. Nothing moved. Yet Crow could swear his heartbeat was loud enough to cover any sounds close at hand.

Tomas gasped in deep breaths, trying to steady his hammering heart as he rose unsteadily to his feet. The crow shook out his feathers and tipped an eye up to where he stood on the floor, then hopped up and over to the workbench, flicking his wings back smartly as if to say he was done with that nonsense. He had never seen a crow attack a raven directly and was stunned by the bird's defense of him.

"We have to go," Tomas said. "And quickly." He reached under the workbench and pulled his automaton from its hiding place, holding it tight.

He crept down the stairs, holding his breath as he sidled past his master, whose vacant eyes glared up at him unblinking, yet accusing him of murder most foul. Once past the ghastly scene, Tomas gently wound his device and placed it on the floor in front of the door.

Crow flew down the stairs and surprised him by landing on his shoulder, cocking his head this way and that as the device unfurled, eight legs expanding out as it stretched up the door jamb and crawled with its mechanical spider grace, tiny sharp tines at the end of each leg holding it firmly in place as it labored higher. When it touched the first lock, it swung its body around, tiny gears whirling as it extruded fine metal pins and nestled against the keyhole.

Tomas held his breath as it worked, clicking and rotating as it puzzled out the lock with its clockwork pattern of actions. There was a loud clunk as the first lock released. The spider sped upward, clasping the second lock and releasing it in less time than the first, and it conquered the next even faster. And the next and the next. When it found no more, it crawled down the door and back to where it had started.

Crow cawed loudly and swooped down to examine the little device.

"Crow, leave it!" Tomas shouted, reaching out to carefully pick up the automaton and slide it into his pocket. Crow cawed again and hopped back up onto his shoulder, reminding him that the bird was probably just hungry.

Just hungry. As he would be once again without a home and back on the streets, just like the hundreds of children with no parents of their own.

Tomas pondered his options as he fed the crow and ate everything he wanted to eat in the kitchen. And when he was done thinking it all through, he laboriously pushed the fat man's body across the floor and down into the basement, where he buried him and his hateful raven as deep as he could through the next day. Then he began to create his new role as the apprentice of a man who had gone away to the country for his health and take care of the clients he had left behind by delivering the items requested, faithfully noted in the man's appointment book.

A Careful Application of Fish

Dana Fraedrich

You might think a mission to locate and steal treasure from inside a small, wooden ship would be easy. Except for two very important things:

That ship is locked up tight inside a much larger building.

And, more importantly, things get tricky when you're stuck inside the body of a raven.

Granted, I'm not cursed with this body all the time. Only during the day. When the sun goes down, however, I change back into a woman. That was the crux of my brilliant plan. I'd sneak in as a raven before sundown and then wait to leave under the cover of dark in my human form with treasure in hand.

The ship, a schooner by the name of the *Gold Bug*, lived up to its name. Throughout the afternoon, I'd watched it sail into port, gleaming with a golden sheen under the bright, tropical, southern sun of my home-city — Bone Port.

The bulk of the city is shaped a bit like a chubby crescent moon, which hugs the clear, green-blue waters of Bone Bay, which in turn, is full of smaller islands that speckle the inlet like stars. Ships coming into and leaving our fair shores have to navigate around these islands. That gave me plenty of time to fly over to the Gold Bug and discretely ensconce myself amidst the sails.

Ravens are neither common nor native to these tropical climes, and while there are plenty of tropical seabirds with black plumage, any sailor worth their salt wouldn't mistake me for a gull or a tern and certainly never a cormorant. And nor do I think anyone would have guessed that I was really secretly a human, cursed to live my days in this avian form, but ravens are extremely clever and have been known to have been utilized for espionage. This is an important factor, given how Bone Port, along with the rest of the continent to the north, was at that time ensconced in a bit of an all-out civil war, but that is a story for another time. Suffice to say, thus was my reasoning for perching atop the gaff of the mainsail rather than below on the railing. Had I chosen to risk being seen, things might not have gone so completely wrong.

In my defense, however, I'd been warned to take care. The treasure I was after reportedly had the simultaneous ability to help fund our war efforts and cripple a large segment of our enemy's forces. Jupiter, the man who'd hired me for this mission, had said to be on the lookout for lots of hired muscle.

Well, technically, he'd said, "Calandra, my sources say the target is protected by the best security money can buy. You're one of my top operatives, so do me a favor and don't get yourself killed."

Jupiter was also an incredible spymaster, so he usually said things like, *"Don't get yourself killed,"* and, *"Never assume anything. Always work off of the intel."*

I had to admit, I wasn't impressed with the intel we had. Looking down from my perch high above the deck, everything seemed normal. Having grown up by the sea, I'd spent as much time on boats of all forms and sizes and uses as I had on land—my time bearing this transformative curse notwithstanding. I knew a normally functioning ship when I saw it. And everything about the Gold Bug was tediously ordinary.

The figurehead was, instead of some great beast or daring warrior, a scarab beetle. Not the most imposing sight to behold on the high seas, but the *Gold Bug* was *allegedly* only a simple merchant vessel, so it didn't need to strike fear into the hearts of enemy combatants. And the captain, one Hortense Bridlepath, had a reputation for running a tight ship. The distinct lack of shilly-shallying amongst her crew bore that out. The only strange part was why a simple merchant vessel needed to be locked securely inside a ship hangar, which was where the Gold Bug currently headed. But while that might raise some eyebrows, money talked and could easily convince those eyebrows to raise themselves at other things. Word of those payoffs had been what tipped Jupiter off to something being amiss about the *Gold Bug* and its cargo.

I was so busy puzzling over all the suspicious things *not* happening below me on deck I'd forgotten to keep an eye on my surroundings. Those of you who possess even the merest sliver of nautical experience may see where this is going. I mentioned previously that I'd perched atop the gaff of the mainsail. For the non-nautically inclined, a gaff is basically a rod that sticks out from the mast to help support and steer a sail. And while schooners like the *Gold Bug* are on the smaller end of sea-going vessel types, they are often still riddled with smaller, extra sails on top. While I was distracted by how bloody normal everything below was as the *Gold Bug* threaded its way around our star field of small islands and sandbars, the topsail swung around and smacked into me like a cricket bat into a ball.

With a grating *caaaaaaaaw!* I arced through the air, spinning, flapping wildly, and failing to catch the wind beneath my wings. I plonked into the water with a… well, a *plonk*. And then debated staying there because, even though the sailors above would never be able to identify me as anything but a stupid bird, that doesn't make getting hurled so spectacularly into the sea any less humiliating. I bobbed to the surface, coughed the water out of my lungs—yes, birds do cough—and listened for any indications that my cover had been blown. Nothing more than raucous laughs, reenactments, and a few bets as to whether or not I was dead met my ears.

Fantastic work, Calandra, I thought sourly. But I was still on a mission and didn't feel much like drowning. My curse protects me from death, but even so, I didn't fancy the experience. And so, since ravens can't really swim, I doggedly extended my wings, flared my tail feathers above the water, and allowed the current to carry my feathery floating body to the nearest bit of land—one of the aforementioned islands. On the way, I did my best to keep an eye on the *Gold Bug* and watched as deckhands helped pull the small vessel, via numerous guide ropes, into the hangar… way, *way* off in the distance at the edge of Bone Port's mainland.

It looked like a giant enjoying a canapé, given that the hangar was usually reserved for much larger ships, like galleons and carracks. As a steam-powered winch hauled the colossal doors shut, sliding them along rollers set into the top of that gaping entrance, the gold sheen of the *Gold Bug* cooled to a pale green. I imagined I could hear the sounds of the entrance sealing up tight, locking me out.

Though I grumbled the whole way, like the good little spy I was, I used the time I spent floating to re-strategize. My unexpected delay was eating up daylight and, therefore, my time as a raven. I was in real danger of losing my avian advantage.

As soon as my talons touched the sandy seafloor, I hustled the rest of the way out of the water and shook myself off. The sun was only minutes from setting! And my feathers had gotten rather sodden during my misadventure. I could feel the same familiar energy of my impending transformation waking inside of me. I shook again and again, trying and failing to take off. But I'd almost managed it! Blazes, this would be much harder if I had to break into the boat hangar as a human.

The island I'd floated to was small, hardly big enough for anything but a fishing stop. A couple of kayaks were moored to a post nearby.

Travel between Bone Bay's islands is possible via a spiderweb-like network of bridges, but kayaking was often faster. The city provided small, one or two-person public ones like these for people to use as needed. More importantly, however, some came with a sort of cloth booster seat to keep one's bottom from getting wet, as kayaks tend to collect water in that area. Often these are just folded lengths of cloth that can double as blankets or what have you—we Bone Portis are a clever and practical bunch.

I half-hopped and half-fluttered over to the small vessels, still trying to dislodge water from my wings as I went. The first kayak didn't have what I was looking for, but the second… Yes! Thank the stars! So, doing my best *not* to think about how many different bums had used it and how long it had probably been since the thing had been laundered, I hopped onto the cloth and began rolling around.

Sunset was so close. Even if I could take off, I didn't know if I'd have time to make it to the boat hangar. There was nothing for it; I had to go *now*. In one… well, not smooth motion, but in one great heave of tumbling effort, I righted myself and launched upward. The sandy ground below consumed my view, and I worried I might have overcorrected. But the wind was on my side now. A gust of briny sea-smelling air wafted under me, and I was off.

Only a thin slice of sun shone its light across the landscape below me—paths paved with crushed seashells and long, low buildings, many sporting huge bleached whale bones as part of their architecture. I flapped harder. My flight ate up the distance between the boat hangar and me, but *how* to get inside? There! Up top, near the roof of the building, small barred windows dotted the perimeter. Probably for ventilation. Bone Port is certainly a tropical paradise, but no one wants to be inside one of its buildings without a cross-breeze going. The openings between the bars were far too small for any human, but a raven could certainly fit.

The song of my transformation was already practicing its scales, nearly ready for its evening performance. Now, if I didn't make it, I'd have a whole new set of problems to contend with: I'd end up splatted against the ground or, even more embarrassingly, against the side of the boat hangar itself.

Almost there...

And only the barest sliver of the sun winked at me from above the horizon. At the very last second, I snapped my wings against my body and pointed my beak toward the space between two bars in one of the windows. Success! I sailed through the gap, opened my wings again, and wheeled around, searching for a safe place to land.

I felt the moment the sun donned his cap for the night and disappeared. In that same instant, light began to emanate from my body.

No, nooo, nonononononono! I thought. *Not now!*

My feathers disappeared and became the clothing I'd been wearing when dawn broke that morning, and my wings stretched, becoming arms. My talons flattened and turned to toenails while my beak shrank and softened. Gravity, harsh mistress that she is, pulled at me. I barely managed to grab a rafter on my way down and swallowed a yelp as I felt my arms consider popping out of their sockets. They decided against it in the end, thank heaven, and I was left hanging several hundred feet in the air.

Good news, the *Gold Bug* was right below me. So close!

Too close, in fact. If I let go here, I'd either end up a greasy stain on the deck or impaled on one of the masts. Thus, I simply shimmied my way down the rafter, trod through bird droppings on the way, and plunged into the water around the ship.

No one was around, as far as I could see. No one had shot a crossbow bolt at me yet anyway, so that was nice.

The building was simple, nothing more than a hollow wooden box with jetties constructed around where boats were meant to dock. The giant doors sat off to one side of me, and in the wall on the other was a human-sized door.

Despite my best efforts to streamline my body into the most tapered shape possible, the splash was enormous. I waited underwater, listening for any cries from someone I might have failed to spot. Silence. I risked peeking my head above water. Still nothing. Excellent.

And so, I began to snoop. Snooping is, by far, my favorite part of the job. I found it almost calming following a process, mentally ticking off boxes. I am neither messy nor a fool, and I didn't want anyone to know I'd been here almost as much as I wanted to find the treasure. Sadly, I found nothing saucier than crew rosters, accounting ledgers, and shipping manifests in the captain's quarters. She even kept everything conveniently tidy and well-labeled. Granted, any of it could omit or disguise information, but I'd need more clues to suss it out.

More clues, of course, beyond this whole ridiculous arrangement—hiding the ship inside a hangar big enough for at least six more schooners of its size. The merchant in charge, if indeed that's what they were, might have paid off the captain to ask no questions. But that wasn't my job to discover. Jupiter had other agents assigned to chat with—or chat up, depending on the situation—the *Gold Bug*'s crew and officers. They'd draw out what information they could from that end.

I scoured every inch of the captain's quarters for secret hiding places. Then the galley, then the crew quarters. Jupiter had bought me extra time. He'd… incentivized the port master to give the *Gold Bug*'s captain a hard time, administratively speaking. Nothing more than some paperwork irregularities. And do you know what I found in all my careful searching? Bloody nothing! Or at least nothing that pointed to anything worth this expense, though I did suspect the ship's cook, or someone in his employ, ran a side business selling "artisanal, open ocean sea salt." That just left the hold to explore.

Getting down was the easy part. True, the hatch was secured with a heavy padlock, but that was nothing my lock-picking skills couldn't handle. All the lanterns down in the hold had been doused. Good. That should mean no nosy crew members down there to complicate things for me. There was a strange smell, however. It wasn't the scent of spoiled food or dry rot. It was a musky, sour sort of smell I couldn't quite place.

The hold, as one might expect, was nothing more than a large, dark, open space for storing goods. I grabbed an oil lamp and adjusted the wick so that it threw just the barest globe of light around me. Everything had been lashed down to keep it from knocking about on rough seas, and whoever had arranged the place had created a sort of warren of crates, dunnage, and barrels. Confusing to navigate, but at least everything could be accessed fairly easily. The cargo, too, had all been labeled, though I didn't trust the labels were all telling the truth. A stack of barrels carrying salted oily fish from the far north smelled right, though, as did some crates of recently tanned hides and other cured animal skins from the same area. I almost thought the latter might be the source of that strange, musky smell that had hit me when I'd first entered the hold. When I got close, however, theirs was a different sort of scent, less fresh.

Nothing on the shipping manifests I'd seen in the captain's quarters had been suspicious, and I couldn't go opening every crate to verify their contents. Crouched low and surrounded by cargo, I allowed myself to let out a soft, frustrated growl.

Another growl, also soft but much deeper answered mine. And it sounded from right next to me.

My blood froze, and I turned my gaze toward the noise.

I knew that sound. I'd heard it plenty of times in the Green Dragon, the huge jungle that hugs the city of Bone Port to the north.

Peering through the gap between two crates at my left, a pair of amber eyes glared at me. The low light of my lantern reflected off sharp, white teeth as the creature pulled its dark lips back in a snarl. A panther. They were native to this area and black as coal. One of nature's most perfect hunters. And all that separated us were a few wooden boxes. I backed away slowly, rising with my back pressed against another wall of cargo. Thank the stars for the boundary between the panther and me, but that wouldn't stop it for long if it was really keen. Suddenly, Jupiter's intel made sense.

The target is protected by the best security money can buy…

A panther couldn't betray you because it was loyal to no one but itself. But it certainly could stab you in the back with those razor-sharp claws.

Bugger. I had no idea how the panther had been captured, but here it was. And, of course, that's where I needed to search. The panther hadn't made a move to climb over the boxes or anything. It just stared at me irascibly through the gap. I wondered when it had last eaten. I wanted to keep track of the creature's location and so decided to scrabble up and over the cargo. Forcing myself to keep going when I eventually had to lose sight of the panther was one of the hardest things I've ever done.

If you've never been stalked by a wild animal, perfectly evolved to rip out your throat before you even know what's happening, allow me to assure you it's the most primal fear you will ever experience. A cold sweat broke out across my skin, and my heart hammered in my chest. Every instinct screamed at me to flee.

"Please don't eat me," I begged under my breath. "For I am stringy and tough and very, *very* bitter. And I will choke you on my way down, so help me!"

False bravado, all. Because, as much as my curse protected me from death, it didn't give my limbs, if severed, any sort of autonomy. It just hurt like hell. I knew that from experience.

Finally, I crested the wall of freight. Only the faint glow of the panther's eyes in my lamplight gave away its position. I couldn't understand why it hadn't come after me—not that I was complaining—until I lowered the lamp further down into the cargo crevasse below me.

Trapped. The poor creature had been blocked in by crates and bound to four of them via short apparatuses of chains, springs, and rods, all attached to a hefty collar. The strange restraints ensured the panther couldn't climb and restricted its range to where the contraption designer wanted it. I actually felt sorry for the creature, as I knew something of how that felt. Sympathy or not, however, I was still on a mission. Countless lives depended on whether or not I succeeded.

A single crate, not topped by any other cargo and not attached to any of the panther's tethers, sat unassumingly in the corner of its prison. The word "Hardtack" was printed across its side, though it was too large to be carried off by a single person. I had a good feeling these features signified its importance. Whoever had masterminded this scheme was clearly too smart to have placed the treasure in something so obvious as an actual treasure chest. The suspiciously unsuspicious crate was also well within reach of the panther's striking distance, though just barely. To me, that indicated they didn't want to risk it being used as a scratching post. Smart, considering the long, deep gashes running down numerous other boxes in the enclosure.

Traveling along the top of the cargo, I found, just outside of the crate-created cage, a trio of catch poles.

Not that helpful. I held no illusions that I'd be able to lasso and control a panther all by myself. Though I wondered for a moment if I might be able to free the creature and lure it on deck. Lure it there without getting my face ripped off, of course. But some, if not all, of the sailors, might be both ignorant and innocent. Surely, they'd all wondered why their little ship had berthed here. And they'd also undoubtedly been told to stop asking so many questions or something equivalent. I was a spy, true, and I had killed, but I was no wanton murderer. Though war comes with casualties, I refused to treat innocent people as disposable.

I sighed. If I were to avoid bloodshed, there was nothing left for it but theatrics. And a careful application of fish.

Theatrics has never been my favorite technique. I like a simple, clean solution. Quiet. Quick. Get in and get out. But when needs must…

I retraced my steps and tipped one of the fish barrels onto its side. The hold had a myriad of tools for ship running, maintenance, and repair scattered all around–bolt cutters, pry bars, fire axe, and more–so it was a simple manner of breaking into the barrel and smashing it up a bit, both to release its salty hoard and make it appear as if the panther had gotten to it. The smell was unreal! Preserved though they were, pounds upon pounds of fish still maintains a strong and distinct redolence. It positively engulfed the musky scent, which I now knew came from the panther.

The beast growled eagerly as I laid a trail leading up to the deck and away from the hatch, ending in a huge pile of fish that would, hopefully, keep the creature occupied for some time.

Finding something to stand in for blood proved more difficult. Red wasn't really part of the Gold Bug's aesthetic, and all the food in the galley tended toward an array of browns and greys. I had to settle for cutting my own arm open and strategically trailing blood down the gangplank near the boat hangar's entrance and painting a few well-placed bloody handprints and smears. It didn't take much so long as I was clever about where and how I placed my warnings. And a little sea water went a long way in making the blood I sacrificed stretch. There, now the possibly-innocent seamen would have plenty of warning as to what awaited them. Though I hoped the panther would escape to the jungle where it belonged.

After bandaging myself up, I hurried back down to the hold for the scariest part of all—releasing the beast. I cut ropes and pushed crates over from above. The panther didn't care for the latter activity one bit. It paced and tugged at its restraints as the heavy cargo crashed to the floor. I sucked a breath in through my teeth, worried someone would hear the commotion. Then, as quickly as I could manage, I reached down with a pair of bolt cutters to start snipping the panther's restraints.

The thing about such a strange system of control is that, as you begin to sever each piece, freedom of movement is restored in equal measure. By the time I'd finished clipping two of the restraints, the panther had doubled its range. Thankfully, I'd done my work in such a way that it still couldn't climb but after this next cut…

The panther paced below me, testing its boundaries with each pass. It eyed the odorous trail of fish I'd made, but its priorities could change in a heartbeat. I kept my eyes on it while I sidled into my next position.

"Now, don't turn on me when I do this," I said in soothing tones. "We'll all be better off if you just toddle off to enjoy your free lunch." I put the tool in position and paused. "To be clear, *I* am *not* the free lunch."

Finally, eyes on the huge, pacing feline, I waited until it was nearly to the end of its path. *Snip!* I could see the moment the panther realized it had more leeway. It redoubled its efforts, tugging at its final restraint as it, most importantly, faced away from me. The final tether, having lost the cooperation of the other three, was no match for such determination. The springs stretched and warped, extending the panther's range yet further. I scuttled to make the final cut. The panther came free with a twang and bounded toward the line of fish.

While it slurped them up like oysters, I hurried toward the so-called hardtack box. Keeping one eye on the freed beastie, though I couldn't lift the box, I could shimmy it forward just enough to get behind it— there was no way I was going to turn my back on the panther. I'd armed myself with a pry bar when I'd picked up the bolt cutters. The panther could be heard gulping its way up the stairs and out the hatch as I pried open what I hoped would prove to be a treasure chest. I did my best to preserve the box's condition to cover my theft.

Inside, I found something rather unexpected.

Rice husks?

Bloody hell, of course. Rice husks were often used as packing material. Stars, what other horrors might fall under "the best security money can buy?" Did venomous snakes lie in wait beneath the husks?

I groaned. I'd already been here far longer than I wanted and needed to get out. I clenched my teeth, cringed, and thrust my hand into the hidden depths of rice husks. My arm swished, buried past the elbow, back and forth through the container. I'd started to think it was empty when my hand found something large and solid… just as several husk-colored spiders, each several inches across, dislodged themselves and skittered in all directions. I let forth a blue streak of swears, grasped the thing, and ripped my arm from the box. Slamming the crate's lid back into place, I trapped the spiders again.

My skin crawled several circuits over itself, and I had to force myself to stay still, listening hard for anyone who might have heard my swearing or slamming. Until it occurred to me that such sounds, while bloodstains decorated around the ship and a panther prowled on deck, would be entirely appropriate. Thus, I stopped worrying about being heard and looked down at what I'd extracted from the spider-infested box.

A crow. A golden crow.

Jupiter sent a *raven* after a *crow*. And a rather gaudy one at that.

The statue had diamonds for eyes and wings encrusted in either onyx or… could it be… *black opals*. Holy blazes, this thing must be worth a fortune! Though I couldn't see how it would help us win the war. Oh well, that was for Jupiter to figure out. It was far too large to fit in my pocket, so I wrapped it in a discarded fragment of material, grabbed a bit of rope I'd cut, and lashed the thing to my torso. I wanted my hands free to carry the pry bar and an axe up to the deck with me, just in case. The lamp hung by its carrying handle gripped firmly between my teeth.

As I passed, the panther was happily gorging itself and barely spared me a glance. The human-sized door I'd seen earlier was locked, but that's where my axe and pry bar came in. I even made a few facsimiles of claw marks on my way out to add to my panther-attack deception.

Proper darkness had fallen by now, and I checked my surroundings before slipping out. I left the door open for the panther. No one was likely to notice too soon, as the inside of the hangar was as dark as the outside. It wasn't a perfect solution. The panther still wore its collar and dragged pieces of the restraints behind it, but I reckoned it'd be better off with that than still trapped.

Later, bedraggled and smelling of fish but triumphant, I arrived in Jupiter's office. When he unwrapped the crow, I got a better look at it.

In the proper light of his office, I could see etchings carved into the bird's back, though what they meant, *if* they meant anything at all, was a mystery.

Jupiter rubbed the dark brown skin of his shaved head. "It's clearly a cryptogram."

"Clearly," I agreed, though it could have just been decorative for all I knew. Puzzles were not my forte.

"Was there anything else stored with it?" he asked. His eyes kept studying the symbols.

"Besides horrifying spiders?" I replied. "No. Not that I found."

Jupiter nodded. "Not surprising. Not like they'd include instructions for cracking the code right next to it." He finally looked at me. "You stink. Go get cleaned up."

I gave him an appreciative nod. "Glad to be of service."

Jupiter said a lot by what he *didn't* say, and I knew he was pleased.

After I'd returned to my own little refuge and washed the reek of fish and fear off of me, I received a note from Jupiter. It was encoded, just as all his communiques were. He'd cracked the golden crow's cryptogram. The thing had opened up to reveal the coordinates of hidden forces, supply cache locations, and plans for an arm of the enemy's naval force. Specifically, the mercenary arm of said force. The crow was going to be their payment. The information inside the crow also named other ships—Hop Frog, Black Cat, Red Death, and more—around the continent that would be carrying more payment and when. At the bottom of Jupiter's note, he'd included a single line that made me smirk ruefully.

I hope you're ready for another mission, Calandra.

Proof of Life or Death

A Machinations Sundry Story

James Chambers

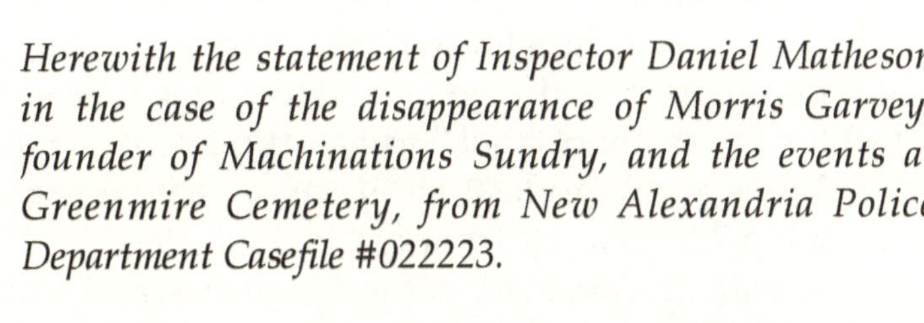

Herewith the statement of Inspector Daniel Matheson in the case of the disappearance of Morris Garvey, founder of Machinations Sundry, and the events at Greenmire Cemetery, from New Alexandria Police Department Casefile #022223.

ON THE DAY OF HIS DISAPPEARANCE, MORRIS GARVEY persuaded me to attend a technology exposition at the Babylon Gardens Exhibition Center. I agreed with reluctance. Wandering for hours to gaze at new industrial gadgets and clockwork butterflies while their makers do their damndest to sell me on their virtues for ushering in the future makes my skin itch. From my years in New Alexandria, I've grown accustomed to city life, but, no secret, I prefer the outdoors and action to cooping myself up among tinkerers and tools. That day, though, I sorely needed a distraction. My investigation into the Diamond Street heists, which coincided with an odd surge in the number of crows on the block, had hit a dead-end when my last lead dried up. I wanted to fret my brain cells over a completely unrelated matter for a while so I could return to the case with fresh eyes. Mr. Garvey's invitation came at an opportune time. I figured to follow him around and let my mind wander. I've gained some of my most useful insights into cases by not thinking about them. Counterintuitive, I know, but don't underestimate the power of the subconscious to show you what you can't see right before your eyes.

The exposition filled the main hall of the Gardens. Loud and damp, full of nonstop chatter and clouds of steam puffing from display models for a bewildering array of mechanized shoe-shiners, oyster-shuckers, looms, and other contraptions. Almost all of them owed a great debt to Morris Garvey, who'd pioneered the miniaturization of steam power with his steam-powered chimney sweeps, blazing a trail for many of these so-called modern conveniences. A majority of the inventors showcasing their wares paid licensing fees for the use of Mr. Garvey's patents. Thus he roamed the aisles like a celebrity. Everyone knew Mr. Garvey, and Mr. Garvey knew damn near everyone.

My detective's trained eye observed their admiration, envy, resentment, and fear. I suspect Mr. Garvey overlooked the range of their regard due to his intense interest in their inventions. He stopped at many of the displays for in-depth demonstrations during which he asked questions, poked at gears, and fine-tuned dials and valves to "get a feel for the steam of it all," as he said. I read the inventors' faces — who gleamed with pride at his attention, who dreamed covetously of dethroning Mr. Garvey from his exalted place in the industry, who smirked with disdain at his earnest inquiries, and who quivered in the presence of greatness to which they aspired but lacked the grit to achieve. Damn colorful bunch, inventors. Full of ideas and anxieties in equal measure, unsure if they wished to make the world a better place or simply make a killing in the market. Mr. Garvey knew all that, but the expo marked a rare pleasure excursion for a man who spent most of his time deep in the labyrinth of the Machinations Sundry shop in downtown New Alexandria, a chance to put aside his own concerns and marvel at the array of ingenuity.

About half past noon, we came to a particularly original and interesting display, the work of one Doctor Ponders K. Sturgeon, a medical man obsessed with a very narrow branch of his trade: death and death-like states, such as catalepsy and paralysis. Dr. Sturgeon's inventions included: a brass lung, a device that straddles a patient's chest to mechanically induce breathing powered by a steam compressor; a steam sterilizer for surgical tools; a steam-driven rapid blood transfusion system, definitely not for the faint-hearted; and his most interesting creation, a steam-powered self-exhuming coffin, the last line of hope for those who feared being buried alive. Until that moment, such a worry had never crossed my mind.

In my experience, especially living in Texas before emigrating to New Alexandria, most people left no doubt about their status when they died because most of the dead folks I encountered met their fate thanks to bullet holes, knife wounds, hangings, poisonings, dynamitings, and skull-crushings under the hooves of one beast or another. The notion of mistakenly burying those folks alive made me laugh. Dr. Sturgeon took exception and delivered an ad hoc lecture, much to my chagrin and Mr. Garvey's delight.

"Why, sir," he said, "have you not heard news of the recent, regrettable discovery concerning the wife of a noted Congressman from Baltimore?"

Mr. Garvey smirked while I admitted ignorance.

"She was stricken by a sudden, paralyzing illness that entirely baffled her doctors. Her attendants tried for days to revive her from her stupor, but all efforts failed. She lingered with her husband and physicians by her side as her pulse weakened and her breath grew shallow, until the day both ceased, and warmth faded from her corpus. They waited still, hours, days, in hope of life's return. Only after she seemed to pass through the unpleasant stiffness of death did her husband abandon all hope and order her buried. A grand funeral followed, concluded with an internment attended by many prominent citizens. None suspected the horrible act upon which they placed their seal. These events occurred some four years ago but only recently achieved notoriety upon the reopening of the lady's family vault to allow the internment of a cousin deceased to typhoid. Dear heavens, my good Inspector, do you know what they found in the vault?"

I cringed as I admitted I did not. Mr. Garvey placed a reassuring hand on my shoulder to, perhaps, remind me that the best inventors wove a degree of showmanship and carnival barker energy into their yakking.

"Why, they found nothing less than the good lady's coffin wide open and the lady herself—her corpse, more precisely—seated atop the coffin of her great-great-grandmother in a pose of sheer despair—and now unquestionably deceased, rendered skin and bone by time, her white cerements grayed by age and dust. They calculated she exited her coffin within a day of her interment, then spent her remaining hours of life struggling to escape her tomb, an impossible feat given its marble-and-steel construction. And yet, all up and down the interior of the door, glints of roughened steel and long-dried blood clots crusted with shards of fingernails demonstrated the fervor of her mad attempts to break free."

A gruesome yarn, and every word of it true, as I later confirmed with my contacts at the *New Alexandria Herald*. Mr. Garvey, of course, knew the tale and delighted in my tortured reaction. Mistaking my morbid curiosity for commercial interest, Dr. Sturgeon continued with example after example of those interred while alive: a young lady in France, rescued when her unrequited lover sought to steal a lock of her hair from her grave and found her alive; a cavalry officer in Leipzig, concussed after falling from his horse, buried, and rescued by the acute hearing of a peasant who sat a while upon his shallow, tree-shaded plot; and a London attorney, dead from an odd case of Typhus, which motivated doctors to hire "resurrectionists" to secure for autopsy his body, which they unexpectedly revived by an experiment in applying galvanic current to the assumed corpse. I tolerated these morbid episodes, delivered with the glee of a campfire storyteller, not out of interest but of patience, for one of the doctor's inventions had secured Mr. Garvey's attention.

The device, displayed anonymously at the back of the doctor's stall, offered hope to those frightful of premature burial that they should never need one of Dr. Sturgeon's self-exhuming sarcophagi. Intended to determine the matter of life or death beyond any doubt, the doctor hoped to place one in every hospital and funeral parlor—just as soon as he perfected it, of course! His Life Detector hadn't yet achieved results reliable enough to mass produce. I deemed the prototype as nothing more than another part of Dr. Sturgeon's sales pitch: "Coming soon, my one-and-only Life Detector to guarantee you're dead before you're buried, but until that miraculous time, don't you need the peace of mind provided by my self-exhuming coffins?" Mr. Garvey, conversely, took it as a challenge and quizzed Dr. Sturgeon down to a level of technical detail that made about as much sense to me as Greek to a bull-steer. He even took out his jade-handled multi-tool, packed with all manner of attachments, such as a screwdriver, a knife, a wire crimper, a magnifying glass, and, especially, a ruler, which he used to measure various parts of the gadget. It satisfied whatever itch Mr. Garvey hoped to scratch that day, though. We departed the exhibition directly after our visit with Dr. Sturgeon and parted ways, Mr. Garvey to the Machinations Sundry shop, and I to NAPD headquarters to throw my attention back to the Diamond Street heists.

I had no further contact with Mr. Garvey that day and thought no more of our visit to the exposition until noon the following day when Andy Parker, a boy of fifteen, one of Mr. Garvey's Sundry Troubleshooters, came to my office in a troubled state. Mr. Garvey assembled this loose-knit group of youths, such as Mr. Parker, after his steam-powered chimney sweeps put so many boys out of work. The group has since grown, its members acting as Mr. Garvey's eyes and ears throughout the city in return for financial help and support toward bright futures. Andy reported that Mr. Garvey had missed their morning appointment, a weekly breakfast, at which Mr. Garvey kept tabs on Mr. Parker's well-being. He held such meetings with all his Sundry Troubleshooters and never missed one. A dozen more youths too shy to speak to me lurked outside my door, eavesdropping, equally anxious over this uncharacteristic lapse. Andy insisted something untoward had befallen Mr. Garvey, requiring immediate action by the NAPD.

Mr. Garvey, being an adult and possessed of a substantial fortune, might simply have gone off on some errand or fancy and found himself detained or distracted, I noted, but Andy refused to accept it. Mr. Garvey never missed an appointment with a Troubleshooter without sending word. There is, I suggested, a first time for everything. Andy scoffed. Grumbles from the Troubleshooters in the hallway agreed. I hollered them all into my office, as motley a crew of boys and girls as I've ever seen. Each, though, possessed a thing most street urchins lack: *hope*. Mr. Garvey had given them that and earned their affection and loyalty, which made their regard for his well-being all the more compelling. I confess, as well, I'm a sucker for two things: a lady in distress and a frightened child.

I promised to look for Mr. Garvey immediately and directed the Troubleshooters to keep watch for any sign of him, with orders to report it to me immediately. After they left, I put on my hat and jaunted downtown to Machinations Sundry headquarters. I half-expected to find Mr. Garvey there, his sleeves rolled up and his hands buried in the gears of some new machine or marvel. But no one had seen him at all that morning. One of Machinations Sundry's chief steam techs, Avram Bordell, who looked as if he'd slept overnight at his workstation, reported that Mr. Garvey spent yesterday afternoon shuttered in his personal workshop, tinkering with some idea that seized his imagination—until evening, when he hurried out with rolls of blueprints and designs tucked under his arm, saying only that he'd discovered the answer to "life or death." No one at the shop reported seeing Mr. Garvey after that time.

I next called on some of Mr. Garvey's close acquaintances. Madame Marceline Rene, who'd returned from Paris that morning, knew nothing of his whereabouts; she fervently wished to aid in my search, but a touch of flu caught at sea kept her bedridden. I discovered Anna Rigel, Queen of New Alexandria's witches, out of town on an extended sabbatical to New Orleans and unreachable. The painter, Edward W. Scott, Mr. Garvey's childhood friend, had not left his studio in days and frowned at my interrupting a session with his favorite model, one Ms. Tessie Reardon. He hadn't spoken to Mr. Garvey for a week. Regular check-ins by Andy Parker and other Sundry Troubleshooters failed to dish up any clues. I grew as apprehensive about Mr. Garvey's situation as them. One lead yet remained. Although it struck me as poor, I've cracked more than a few cases by delving into every possibility, however tenuous and unlikely.

Around 7 p.m. that evening, I knocked upon the door to Dr. Ponders K. Sturgeon's home, a brownstone at 1113 East Kipps Street. Mr. Garvey had left Machinations Sundry speaking of "life or death," recalling to me his keen interest in Dr. Sturgeon's flawed Life Detector. Perfecting it and presenting his solution to its creator fell square within Mr. Garvey's typical behavior, one of the blind spots in his social skills, as he always expected a warm, grateful reception to his, in effect, showing up a competitor or colleague. A gray-haired butler answered the door and led me to an ostentatious parlor. Dr. Sturgeon owned the entire building. Steam lungs and self-exhuming coffins paid quite well, it seemed. Garbed in a soiled surgical apron, the doctor himself soon joined me, pouring us each a glass of brandy, which, being on duty, I sniffed but didn't drink. He displayed concern for Mr. Garvey but said he hadn't seen or spoken to him since we departed the exhibition hall the previous afternoon. I asked how he might take it if Mr. Garvey appeared at his door with solutions to his Life Detector's glitches.

"I'd be overjoyed," he said. "Think how many minds it would put at ease; all the poor souls spared the torture of premature burial. We inventors have no egos when it comes to making the world a better place."

A more aromatic line of bull-pucky I've rarely heard. At yesterday's exhibition, where Mr. Garvey saw only machines and potentialities, I'd observed nothing but egos. I posed to Dr. Sturgeon a series of questions on a wide range of topics about his work and habits in hopes of detecting inconsistency or hesitation in his answers. He replied convincingly without fail. While we spoke, Dr. Sturgeon fidgeted, his hands in constant motion, whether swirling his brandy, gesturing to make a point, or reaching into his apron pockets to fiddle with the implements stored there. Anxiety, clear and simple, but over what? How much of his business did his self-exhuming coffins comprise, I asked. He demurred on details, but a minute smirk at the left corner of his mouth hinted at the nerve I'd struck. He concluded our friendly chat, then summoned his butler to show me the door. I departed, my concern for Mr. Garvey deepening. Dr. Sturgeon had something to hide, no doubt about it, but what? My line of questioning had only opened up myriad new possibilities when one considered how many of the inventors at the exposition eyed Mr. Garvey with envy or disdain.

Two blocks from Dr. Sturgeon's home, Andy Parker approached me, running hard with a girl perhaps a year younger than him on his heels. Andy introduced me to Gabriella Martini, a Sundry Troubleshooter in good standing, and pled with me to hear her report. She had seen a strange sight yesterday but hadn't understood its importance until speaking with Andy. Around 8 p.m. the prior evening, going by the bells of St. Dominic's, she happened to pass by Dr. Sturgeon's house at the same time Mr. Garvey, with a bundle of papers clutched in his arms, had entered it, welcomed by the butler. She didn't see him depart, but close to midnight, found herself on the next block as she walked home from an evening job Mr. Garvey had arranged for her at the Egyptian embassy. Three "rough-looking men" nearly rammed her as they pulled a cart from an alley mouth that adjoined the backlot of Dr. Sturgeon's house. Dirty canvas hid its bulky payload. The men ignored her, but as the cart jounced to the cobblestone street, an item bounced from its bed: a jade-handled multi-tool engraved with the initials: MG. When she presented it to me, I recognized it without hesitation. I'd seen Mr. Garvey use it on the previous afternoon.

Applauding Gabriella for recovering it, I bid Andy to canvas the Troubleshooters for anyone else who might have seen the cart. Then I returned to Dr. Sturgeon's brownstone. After studying the building and its grounds front and back, I concealed myself in a shadowy niche along the alley. It afforded me a clear sight of the home's back windows, door, and ground-level cellar entrance, covered by steel doors set on a gentle slope. The picture forming in my mind offered little optimism. I now knew Mr. Garvey had entered Dr. Sturgeon's home the prior evening. I had no evidence he'd ever exited. Dr. Sturgeon, an obvious egotist, had lied to me and hid what he knew of Mr. Garvey's activities from the time in question. Mr. Garvey, I suspected, had fixed the doctor's Life Detector then arrogantly presented his findings, only for Dr. Sturgeon to snap and either harm, imprison—or, perish the thought, murder— Mr. Garvey to steal them and present them as his own work.

Hours passed with little activity inside Dr. Sturgeon's house. Twice, members of the Troubleshooters passed by the mouth of the alley, but I kept my concealment. I hoped that Dr. Sturgeon, rattled by my visit and probing questions, would take some action to expose himself. At midnight, two men wheeled a cart into the mouth of the alley. The hunch of their shoulders and the basso resonance of their footfalls revealed the weight of their burden. They stopped at the back of Dr. Sturgeon's house. The butler opened the door and lit a gas lamp hanging there, casting an unsteady orange sheen on the men and their delivery. He regarded them with disdain, then gestured to the cellar doors mounted in the ground. One man sprang down from the cart and stamped his foot three times on the lefthand door. Seconds later, both doors creaked and clanged open. Dr. Sturgeon rose upon what I presume were stairs connected to his cellar, his surgical apron more thoroughly mottled by apparent bloodstains and his hair disheveled.

"What have you brought me?" he asked the men.

They drew back the canvas, revealing a most hideous sight: three corpses. A young man in soldier's garb, a middle-aged woman in a fine lace dress, and a child in pauper's attire. All of them displayed the sallow, sunken eyes and gray flesh of the grave. Removing the canvas unleashed a cloud of unholy odor that set my eyes watering. My heart broke for the dead as much as my stomach churned. Worse still, Dr. Sturgeon's indifference lit a rage in me when he eyed the corpses like a housemaid eyeing fish in the market, then scolded the men for the lack of "freshness of the specimens." He needed bodies in lesser states of decay to properly conduct his research. He offered the "resurrectionists" half their asking price and refused to haggle. Their collective callousness incensed me. I reached to my holster, ready to draw my Colt, dead-set on wrangling all four men red-handed, certain it would offer me ample leverage to wrest the truth about Mr. Garvey from Dr. Sturgeon. Before I could step from the shadows, though, a powerful blow connected with the back of my head and jarred me from neck to toes. As I spun into a swirling blackness, it came to me that Gabriella had reported three men, not two. One had hung back on lookout. They had gotten the best of me.

I woke in the most unpleasant of confinements: a coffin. I knew it by its shape, which tapered from shoulders to feet, and by the fine silk padding upon which I lay. It rocked and bumped as the cart which carried it trundled over cobblestones, dirt, and gravel. Through gaps where the lid imperfectly joined the sides, the night sky and stars peeked in at me. I estimated the length of my unconsciousness at no more than one hour. The bells of St. Dominic's rang once, confirming this and alerting me by their distant sound to roughly how far I'd traveled. When the cart stopped, I guessed we'd reached Whittaker Pier, going by the soft clang of buoy bells and lapping water.

Hands invisible to me lifted my coffin. Voices grunted and swore at the burden as they stowed me on a barge or another kind of small boat. I hollered for them to free me, to spare themselves the harsh punishment for kidnapping an Inspector of the NAPD. I swiveled my wrists and pushed against the lid, which refused to budge. The coffin fit my broad shoulders too tightly for me to turn or twist more than inches. I kicked at the bottom and butted the lid with my forehead. Nothing gave, nothing moved. The men ignored me. Our vessel lolled into the East River. Paddles splashed and dripped with a steady rhythm. I carried on urging the men to do the right thing and release me, promised them a good word if they helped me square away the real villain, Dr. Sturgeon. No response came. When we completed our crossing, invisible hands again lifted my prison and bore it to a waiting cart. Wood scraped as they slid me into place. My journey continued.

Dr. Sturgeon's vivid, almost gleeful descriptions of premature burials echoed through my thoughts. The sad stories of souls discarded before their time, of suffering unknown by anyone but them. My pulse surged. Sweat beaded my brow. I prayed for the bumping and rocking of the cart to never end. As long as it continued, I remained above ground. But end, it did. The cart sat motionless for a period of time I couldn't measure. I cried out and wrestled for some purchase to give me leverage to thrust myself out against the lid, but the damn coffin fit me like an oak suit two sizes too small. The scrape of iron against dirt taunted me. I tried not to picture the deepening hole the sound suggested. Then my container tilted as my captors lifted and carried me. They argued over the best way to rig ropes to lower me, revealing in the process that they were placing my coffin atop the one they'd emptied of the soldier's body earlier that night. My descent followed only moments later.

Soil and rocks scraped the sides of my coffin. Dirt rained down on my lid. The lowering motion ceased, and the drizzle turned to a downpour as they shoveled great heaps of earth onto me. Streams of dust and grit leaked through the imperfectly fitting lid. The scattered thudding of each new load grew more muted as the layer deepened above me. Did I occupy one of Dr. Sturgeon's self-exhuming coffins? I had no idea. I cursed myself for not paying closer attention to his damnable sales pitch when he showed me how it functioned. I banged on the lid and shouted. The voices of the "resurrection men" grew faint as load after load of soil increased the distance between me and the surface world.

At once the sounds from above ceased. I lay trapped within the literal quiet of the grave.

I resisted the despair trying to overwhelm me and set my mind to seeking escape. The air thinned. Or maybe my fear made it seem so. I fought for my composure, but I couldn't trust my senses. Filled with dread and disoriented, I imagined the entire world lay atop me, crushing me, erasing me from existence. Squeezed into a space too small for my husky body, I felt like a mouse stuck in the throat of a snake. My thoughts cycled through one useless idea after another before it occurred to me to practice the breathing control I'd learned long ago when I competed as a free-diver in the Gulf of Anahuac. Calm returned, but it brought with it no new possibilities, only the cold prospect of acceptance. I couldn't turn or reach out in any way for help. The fatal outcome of my predicament seemed certain.

Then the dirt shifted. The scrape of metal against pebbles, sand, and clay resumed. With each shuffle of soil and iron, the load upon me seemed to lighten rather than deepen. A nightbird's song trickled into my ears, the very sweetest of sounds. My coffin lurched. It rocked and jerked and slammed me against one side and then the other. It jolted upright, forward, upright, forward, upright, bashing my face against the lid with each clumsy motion. A flurry of pulsing mechanical noises clattered in my ears. The wild ride carried on, battering my senses until the scrape of dirt finally ceased, and my coffin stood motionless. The lid of my prison creaked. Its gaps widened. I gasped to catch my breath, then prepared for the one chance I might receive. Fingers appeared beneath the lid's edges as hands yanked it to the side. I thrust myself outward with all the force my cramped, aching muscles could summon and pummeled a man to the ground. As I raised my fist to mash his nose against his skull, I recognized both his voice and face.

I stared down at Morris Garvey.

"Fancy meeting you here, Dan," he said.

I pulled myself off him and clambered to my feet, then helped him to stand beside me.

Panting on the side of my erstwhile grave, I tried to make sense of the vista that greeted me. My three captors, Dr. Sturgeon's resurrectionists, lay flat on the ground, unconscious, victims of timely shovel-blows to the back of the head, as Mr. Garvey later informed me. My coffin, indeed one of Dr. Sturgeon's self-exhuming models, protruded from loose soil like an unkempt grave marker. A spidery assortment of mechanized claws, diggers, and limbs sprouting from it, evidence of its function, not that I can explain it. A few yards away, a second identical coffin stood in an identical position from its own recently excavated burial.

"How about that?" Mr. Garvey said. "We have matching coffins."

The picture I'd formed of Mr. Garvey's fate inside Dr. Sturgeon's house had missed the bullseye but not by much. Mr. Garvey had gone to Dr. Sturgeon with the key to perfecting his Life Detector and found the doctor a surprisingly unwilling collaborator. Mr. Garvey had left the doctor's house in the same manner as I did, locked within one of Dr. Sturgeon's patented coffins. Mr. Garvey demonstrated in his coffin where Dr. Sturgeon had removed all of the control mechanisms from within reach of its cargo, rendering it inoperable. Or so the doctor thought. Mr. Garvey saw it as a puzzle. How to access the fundamental mechanisms still in place with no tools and no light? It took him hours, but he succeeded, and none too soon, as his air supply had nearly run out. Miraculous, in my opinion, but a task that Mr. Garvey described as "a simple matter of crossing the right wires and banging on the right tubes." He admitted, though, a stroke of good fortune in the resurrectionists' poor job of burying him, which left the soil loose enough for the coffin's in-built steam motor to function without clogging or overloading. The abrupt emergence of his sarcophagi from the earth had rattled the resurrectionists, superstitious men who believed the dead were coming to life for retribution. Mr. Garvey advantaged their surprise to take them on with a shovel. He then cobbled together pieces from his coffin to repair mine and activate its self-exhuming functions by means of a feed he snaked through my heavy earth covering.

"We robbed our own graves," he said, "and you didn't even have to lift a shovel to do it. Isn't technology grand?"

I expressed in colorful but restrained language how my perception of events differed from Mr. Garvey's. After securing Dr. Sturgeon's body snatchers with rope from their own cart, Mr. Garvey and I hiked to the caretaker's shack on the far side of Greenmire Cemetery. The man turned white at the sight of us but achieved some color in his cheeks when I showed him my NAPD badge. He directed us to the nearest NAPD station, one mile away, where I dispatched men to formally arrest the resurrectionists and more men to carry word to NAPD headquarters to monitor Dr. Sturgeon's home. Mr. Garvey and I then commandeered an NAPD coach and returned to the heart of the city.

Together we oversaw a pre-dawn raid of Dr. Sturgeon's home that resulted in the arrest of the doctor and his butler and the discovery of a shocking array of experimental medical devices beyond the pale of rational medicine, numerous corpses in varying states of dissection, a handful of terrifying devices intended to animate dead limbs, and a trove of notebooks and ledgers that exposed Dr. Sturgeon's criminal activities going back several years. Most shocking of all, Mr. Garvey demonstrated for me that Dr. Sturgeon's Life Detector did, in fact, work flawlessly as intended—but the doctor refused to bring it to the market because his Self-Exhuming Coffins earned him a small fortune each year. Mr. Garvey had confronted him with this discovery, motivating Dr. Sturgeon to bury Mr. Garvey to protect his secret. Possessed of a surplus of his fancy coffins, the doctor had used two that failed his quality control test to send me and Mr. Garvey to our subterranean prisons.

I noted to Mr. Garvey that I'd identified that aspect of Dr. Sturgeon's ploy right off at the Exposition. While he acknowledged my intuition, Mr. Garvey said, "But you couldn't prove it. It took both of us working together to do that. We make a good team." For the record, while I appreciate all of Mr. Garvey's actions and testimony, which has proven essential in the prosecution of Dr. Sturgeon and his gang, I personally do not consider being buried alive in neighboring graves as the benchmark for what makes a good team.

On the plus side, though, I briefly turned the tables on Mr. Garvey's ingenuity when I blurted out "Crows can count!", leaving him baffled. The notion arriving out of the blue, or, should I say, out of the depths of my subconscious when my brain's quiet workings illuminated the significance of the crows spotted daily along Diamond Street, so obvious I'd overlooked it. For Mr. Garvey's benefit, I explained my realization. The crows counted the comings and goings of the jeweler then reported to the robbers, who'd trained the feathered nuisances to case the joint. Thus they knew when to strike for the largest possible score. If I followed the crows, they would lead me to the criminals. Although it helped me solve the Diamond Street heists, I cannot recommend premature burial as a regular part of police procedure.

Annabel Lee

Jessica Lucci

ANNABEL'S SINGING LURED THE CROW CLOSER, HER VOICE soft and breathy, like an ocean zephyr whispering in through the porthole of the exorbitant cruise ship.

> Oh, little crow,
> What do you know
> Of the land beyond the sea
> What can you tell me?

The crow hopped next to her, where she idled in her bed, and dropped a small ruby brooch onto the thick quilt. "Annabel Lee," it cawed in a soft cracking voice.

"You roguish creature," Annabel laughed. "Thank you for the gift, though we must try to return it to whomever you stole it from."

The door adjoining her boudoir to the captain's chamber door swung open. Captain Edgarton entered carrying a silver breakfast tray with a small pot of tea. The smile slid from his face when he drew in the scene. He abruptly thumped the tray onto a large, polished chest.

"I told you, I do not approve of this dratted flying rat, especially in your private chambers! It probably carries fleas, and I do not need to subject my guests to vermin! Disgusting, vile creature!"

The crow looked inquisitively from the captain to Annabel.

"The crow was only bringing me a shiny trinket. See?" Annabel held up the ruby brooch.

The captain roared. "A thief, that one! It would pluck the twinkle from my eye if it could! What would our guests say if they knew that their property was being stolen by a nasty bird!" He stepped closer and waved at the crow wildly. "Away with you!"

Annabel called out, "Goodbye, friend!"

"Friend?" the captain asked incredulously. "What need do you have of friends? That fiend is no friend, anyway."

"But I love it!"

The captain slammed his fist upon the large chest, rattling the breakfast tray. "You are to love only me!"

"Yes, of course," Annabel answered.

"Didn't I name this very vessel for you? The HMS *Annabel Lee*? What prouder exclamation of my devotion to you could you need? And yet you are amused by a filthy flea instead of focusing your attention on me."

Annabel rolled down the quilt from her lounging body and smoothly slid her legs over the edge of the bed so that her bare toes barely touched the wooden floor. She arose and reached her arms out to her fiancé.

"Of course, I would like to give you my attention. I admire the proclamation of dedication you set forth by granting your grand cruise ship my name."

"Remember the day we christened her?" The captain folded his arms.

"Yes, that was a glorious day, indeed." Annabel stepped toward him and placed her slender hands upon his arms. He unfolded them and embraced her.

"Just remember who the captain is," he murmured into her hair.

"Of course," she said. "I will not forget."

"Right then." The captain turned toward the adjoining door. "I will give you the rest of the day to prepare for the Captain's Ball tonight. I am sure you will do me proud." He closed the door behind him.

Annabel stared after him and then sat at her vanity. As she brushed her long black hair, softly, she sang:

> Let not my voice be of lamentation
> And yet instead be of adoration
> For I am to be the bride and queen
> To the illustrious captain, sea king

At the window, the crow silently listened.

An elaborately fashioned cruise ship, the HMS *Annabel Lee* held the glamourous job of ferrying the most genteel guests from Boston to Barcelona and back again. It was the largest vessel of its kind, much adored by not only the captain but by his steadfast crew, diligent out of pride and out of fear of Captain Edgarton's fiery temper. He was rumored to have thrown at least one cabin boy overboard. Nobody wanted to test that theory.

The grand ship was joyous, a pleasure cruise for the genteel wealthy who needed a diversion from their gilded lives. They left their castles and mansions to what some members of the press referred to as "The Kingdom of the Sea." If it was a kingdom, then Captain Edgarton was its king. And his betrothed, Annabel Lee, namesake of the hulking palace on water, was the queen.

The guests, as the captain referred to his passengers, adored the ship. It was ordained in an almost mythical ornateness, with Greek columns in the dining room and authentic masterpieces adorning the walls. Velvet curtains lined the long broad cabin windows. The salty air was that of joy, of decadence, of freedom.

Annabel Lee, the ship's namesake, was beautiful in an exotic way rather than an extravagant way. She was small and slender, with tiny feet and long fingers. She dressed modestly, yet not without ornamentation; she wore her fascinators like crowns and indeed moved with the dignity of a princess.

The night of the ball felt especially illustrious. Edgarton was obsessed with the cleanliness of the ship, polishing the handrails as he walked the deck with Annabel beneath a purple twilight sky. Guests bowed and curtsied to the captain and Annabel as if they were royalty, even though many of them were peers themselves.

Annabel heard the distinct but subtle rustle of feathers above the gentle din of dark rolling waves. Just ahead, the crow had settled on the handrail and waited as if in anticipation. Annabel stopped and greeted the bird. "Hello, friend."

Captain Edgarton hissed. "What will my guests think?"

"Annabel Lee," the bird cawed, dropping a brass button at her feet. The captain bent over to pick it up, as Annabel could not as tightly corseted as she was. He clutched the button in his hand, swung his arm back, and aimed, throwing it straight at the crow. The brass caught the light of the rising crescent moon just as the crow dodged it, and it fell into the sea.

"Annabel Lee," the crow repeated before flying off into the night, blending into the deepening sky.

The ball was off to a superb start, with a classical orchestra playing lilting songs on a calm sea. At the captain's table were the usual dukes and duchesses, other would-be royalty, lords and ladies, and one very outspoken red-headed woman of a certain age. Madame Isabelle Sophia d'Avery by name, a round, robust socialite who had earned her place at the table through her vast riches gained in her widowhood. A savvy art collector, she had made herself another small fortune in the art trade. She traveled not only for pleasure but to transport her treasures from port to port for exorbitant sale.

Madame d'Avery wore such a large bustle that she had to sit sideways on her chair. Her face was flushed with laughter in quite an unladylike way, in Captain Edgarton's opinion. "Gadzooks," he whispered to Annabel. "She is telling bawdy jokes."

The table roared with laughter as Madame d'Avery chugged another glass of red wine.

"What hangs at a man's thigh and wants to poke the hole that it's often poked before?"

The titillated group called out all the wrong answers. "Do tell us," urged Annabel. Captain Edgarton groaned.

Madame d'Avery took a large breath, creating a suspenseful pause. Her large bosom threatened to pop out of her rounded bodice. "A key!"

The table erupted in laughter. Edgarton wished there was something stronger than wine in his glass. He nudged Annabel Lee and spoke just barely above a whisper. "Don't laugh. It will only egg her on."

Madame d'Avery had sharp ears and observant eyes. She saw the elbow of the captain meet the thin, silked arm of his fiancée. She heard the words uttered from his mouth.

"We all deserve a good laugh," she said into the air, addressing no one in particular. But she saw the crimson flush of anger start at the base of the captain's throat above his cravat. She knew she had been understood.

After the dinner, the grand ballroom filled with excited dancers, couples and pairs who had met onboard the HMS *Annabel Lee*. The automaton servants even seemed to step more gaily as they attended to their duties.

Masterminded by the greatest engineers, the servants were created to be mechanical soldiers. Yet, in this time of great peace, there was no need for articles of war or fighting metal men. So they were redesigned as workers aboard ships such as the *Annabel Lee*, from automatons feeding coal to the steam engines to the serving staff, rolling on well-oiled wheels with brakes that stopped the progress of the shiny creatures in rough waters. All the details of daily life on board were regulated by clockwork, creating a smooth transition for busy socialites to easy ocean faire.

Annabel excused herself from the hustling swishes of cloth and clogs. She made her way furtively to the deck in search of the cool night air. As she exited the ballroom, she was side-swiped by a large object at her hip.

"Oh! Do pardon me," exclaimed Madame d'Avery. She adjusted her bustle with an easy flounce, causing her entire backside to bounce.

"No need for pardon," Annabel said. "We all suffer for our fashions."

Madame d'Avery eyed Annabel's wasp-like figure. "Some suffer more than others."

"I will say the captain appreciates my efforts, but it does make laughing difficult."

"Then I must ask your pardon again, for I did see you laughing, if only the best you could under the circumstances."

"Under the circumstances, yes," Annabel agreed.

Madame d'Avery hooked her arm with the younger woman's. "Since we both seem headed in the same direction, we might as well hobble together."

Annabel smiled. "Indeed."

The two women stepped out onto a balcony. The dark ocean loomed beneath them, with small cresting waves blinking in the reflection of the starry night.

"Do you not have someone to accompany you?" Annabel asked.

"I have been a widow long enough to be able to navigate the sea solo. Of course, at times, I must remove my glove to pronounce a solid slap across the mug of some more forward of the masculine kind, but as I get older, those occasions have become fewer."

"You are still a looker."

Madame d'Avery guffawed in a deep throaty laugh that Annabel was growing to love. "As long as you and I think so, that's all that matters."

After taking in some air, the chill coaxed the two women back into the ballroom. They pranced arm in arm to the punch bowl.

Captain Edgarton watched disapprovingly from across the room. He excused himself from his conversation and shifted his way across to Annabel. He tugged her elbow, causing her to spill her punch upon the elaborate tablecloth. He grabbed the crystal goblet from her and slammed it down onto the table so that more of the red liquid jumped up and out. He steered her away, his teeth gritted, and his lips pulled back in a false smile. He spoke between the gaps in his mouth.

"What are you doing consorting with that American trash?"

"But *you* are American, too."

"But I am not THAT kind of American. I know my place in the world, and it's time you learned yours." His grip tightened. She shook her arm to remove his hold, but he only tightened his grip. "Don't embarrass me," he growled.

Just then, a brush of wings touched Annabel's cheek. The crow flew between the couple's heads before resting on top of the captain's.

"Annabel Lee" cawed the crow and dropped a silver dessert fork. Annabel caught it before it fell to the floor.

Captain Edgarton yelled out an oath unbecoming of a gentleman. He thrashed at his head, missing the black bird as it took wing and swooped down at him. The orchestra stopped playing, and the crowd strayed from dancing to encircle the feisty scene. Gasps of shock gave way when one throaty voice laughed. Soon the entire ballroom was in hysterics.

"Here, let me help." Annabel reached for the crow, holding the silver fork out like a perch. The captain swatted her away and stabbed himself with the tiny fork in the process.

"You she-dog! You stabbed me!"

The crow flew away, out past the balcony, and into the night.

"I did not mean to," Annabel wailed.

Edgarton heard all the laughter and raised his arms in false joviality. "This ball is for more than just the birds!" His voice rang broadly through the crowd. "Please, continue your festivities!" He grabbed Annabel's waist and whispered seethingly. "As for you, you are taking a break."

He led her back to her quarters and threw her to the floor.

"You wench! How dare you embarrass me in front of my guests! After all I have done for you, this is how you repay me? Consorting with the trashiest of all the people on board my vessel and especially encouraging that confounded bird! I swear I will kill it, mark my words!"

He stomped to the heavy flat chest of oak, his gift to her upon their engagement. Her hope chest. He lifted the heavy lid and, in a flurry of fearsome rage, commenced yanking out the contents, gowns of lace and embroidered silk, beaded bags, and golden fascinators flung with careless violence around the berth. Annabel drew herself to her knees and sobbed.

"Please, stop! My trousseau! My family gave that to me!"

Edgarton stomped over to where she lay huddled. He crouched down and, with a heavy hand, slapped her face so hard her head snapped to one side.

"You deceitful little girl, maybe you should fly off with that rotten thief of a creature you so adore—birds of a feather flock together! I'll send you back to that silky port where I found you!" Finally, the hope chest stood emptied, its contents strewn about the room like morning fog. He left, and Annabel cried softly to herself.

"If only I could
If only he would
Send me back to my home
I would not be alone"

She heard a tapping at her window and drew herself up from the floor. Again, a light tap, soft, patient. Annabel crept to the window and peered into bright ebony eyes. Quietly, she gasped and let the crow in.

"Annabel Lee," it quietly cawed, and one talon opened to drop a gleaming pearl ring into her outstretched hands.

"Thank you, my friend, my only friend."

The door connecting her boudoir to the captain's chamber began to slide open. Annabel shook in fear. "Please, go, fly away, be safe!" she begged of the crow. But it was too late.

An angry shadow doused the flicker of a contrite smile gracing Edgarton's face.

"I come here to ask you back to the ball and find you like this? I told you not to seek out that scurvy devil again!"

"But I didn't! The crow appeared at my window, so I let it in, lest someone on the deck see it!"

"Don't insist on making me a fool! The next time you make me a fool on account of that bird will be your last!"

He chased the crow around the room, trampling on all of Annabel's flouncy treasures. He removed his belt and attempted to whip the bird as it darted around him.

Annabel stepped to the window and cried out. "This way, my friend, here is your escape!"

The crow heeded her advice and bolted out into a sea breeze. Annabel barely had time to take a breath of relief before she turned and saw Edgarton, his formidable form looming over her, his right arm raised with his belt dangling high above his disheveled head. She heard the snap before she felt it sting her cheek.

"Next time will be the last time," Edgarton said with the dead calm of a pending storm. He turned and left, straightening his attire, and headed back to the ball alone.

Annabel stared longingly out the window. As was her habit, she sang through her tears.

What would it be like to
Fly away in the night
What would I have to do
To escape my plight

Annabel slept in disarray, dreaming of black seas and white clouds.

Annabel rose from her vanity and stepped out into the midafternoon light. No sooner had the door closed behind her than she felt a gentle thump against her thigh.

"Oh, excuse me," Madame d'Avery said, spinning around, her buoyant backside bobbing.

"No bother at all," said Annabel, lowering her eyes in shame.

Madame d'Avery frowned and reached a gloved hand to Annabel's chin, tilting her head up. "My word, Mistress Lee, what has he done to you?"

"Nothing," Annabel said hurriedly. "Nothing has happened."

"I wondered where you went to after that delightful romp with the crow last night. Now I see why you did not return." Madam d'Avery's eyes narrowed. "Where is he now? I'll teach him a lesson."

"No, please," Annabel begged. She inwardly cursed herself for not performing a better job with her makeup. "It was my fault. You see, I was tightening my corset, and a taut strap slapped me in the face."

The two women stared at each other, each one's eyes imploring the other to do what they each thought to be the best thing.

Finally, Madame d'Avery reached out both hands and clutched Annabel's. "I will choose to pretend to believe you as long as you know that I know that is not the truth."

Annabel lowered her eyes. "Thank you, Madame d'Avery."

"No need for such formality between us. You may call me Isabelle Sophia."

The younger woman looked up gratefully. "And I insist you call me Annabel."

The two women strolled along the deck, arm in arm. They talked of everything and nothing, and Annabel had to stop several times to catch her breath from laughing. Finally, it was time to attend dinner. A small orchestra—a marvel of automaton instruments—set a soothing mood with bows shifting lightly upon violin strings, metal woodwinds that gained their breath from subtle bellows, and, of course, a player piano, played tunes not meant for dancing.

Annabel halted at the entrance.

"What is it?" asked Madame d'Avery. "Oh, you have not seen him since the incident that never happened, I understand. Well, my dear, what shall we do?"

"I must attend dinner with him. It would be a tremendous embarrassment if I missed the occasion."

"An embarrassment for whom?" said Madame d'Avery, with salt in her voice.

Annabel stiffened.

"Ah yes, we cannot upset our illustrious captain, now, can we? You and I will talk on this matter later, in all truth. But for now, let us have dinner. I am starving after all our chatting."

Annabel glanced at her gratefully.

"And if you like, I can seat myself beside you. Heck with seating arrangements!"

Annabel covered her surprised smile at the older woman's crass language but nodded in agreement.

Annabel was seated next to Edgarton. Not a word was said between them, and he did not bother himself to look at her. He paused his cheerful conversation only long enough to glower at Madame d'Avery.

The servants arrived with trays of food, elaborately placed in front of each guest.

Annabel looked down at her plate and grimaced. She commenced picking at the honey-glazed carrots and scalloped potatoes.

"What is wrong with your appetite, Annabel?" Madame d'Avery gestured to her plate. "You haven't touched your Cornish game hen."

"Do not worry, Isabelle Sophia, I am eating my fill of delicious vegetables. It is just that I no longer eat bird flesh."

Captain Edgarton clanked his silverware to the table. "Preposterous," he said, addressing Annabel for the first time.

"I mentioned that weeks ago," murmured Annabel softly.

"Don't worry, my dear," tutted Madame d'Avery, patting Annabel's hand. "Some people are just afraid of their time to eat crow."

"Is that an insult to me?" growled the captain.

"If the shoe fits…"

Edgarton's face grew red with inert rage. His eyes darted around the table at those unsure what to think of this exchange. He cracked a smile. "The old biddy is up to her pranks again." He forced a laugh. The guests joined him, and the dinner went on to the next course, then to dessert. Madame d'Avery told no jokes that night.

The men moved to the deck to smoke cigars while the ladies remained at the table to chitter chatter over absinthe. Smoke wafted in the open doors between the deck and the dining room. "Excuse me," said Annabel to Madame d'Avery. "I have never appreciated the smell of cigars. I, too, am tired from our long walk today and will retire to my bed chamber."

Through the grey smoke, the black crow glided. It landed at Annabel's feet and tapped its beak on the floor. "Annabel Lee," it cawed and dropped a diamond-encrusted cufflink before her. Madame d'Avery heard the crow's dry voice and hustled over to investigate. She picked up the cufflink and handed it to Annabel. "This crow has good taste."

There was a sound of a scuffle, and Edgarton appeared, smoke encircling his head like coal smoke from a steam engine. His face was as red as raked embers.

"How dare you," he spat. The crow zoomed away, just missing being stomped upon by the captain.

Madame d'Avery watched as Edgarton grasped Annabel's waist and whispered like fire. "As for you, you are taking a break."

He marched to her quarters where her hope chest's promises remained strewn across the floor from his previous tantrum. He closed the door. The music swelled. And the night went on as before.

The next day, the HMS *Annabel Lee* docked joyously in Barcelona. Madame d'Avery sought out Annabel to say farewell. She bumped into people, knocking plates off breakfast tables with her large bustle. She became frantic. She spotted Captain Edgarton.

The captain smiled heartily, standing proudly at the gangplank, accepting praise and gratitude for yet another impressive pleasure cruise. Madame d'Avery stormed over as the captain shook hands with one of his many admirers stepping down to the dock.

"Where is she?"

A dark cloud shaded the captain's features, and his lips curled back into a snarl. "That is none of your concern."

"It is my concern! She is my friend!"

"Ha! She has no friends."

"I'm sure she has you to thank for that. Now, where is she? I insist upon saying goodbye to her."

"You are too late for that," the captain growled quietly.

Madame d'Avery crossed her arms across her broad bosom and planted her feet apart in what the captain deemed unladylike fashion. "I am not leaving this ship until I bid my farewell."

"Farewell to you then!" Edgarton beckoned two large human deckhands toward them. "Please escort Madame d'Avery to shore. It seems she has taken on too much seawater and needs to dry out."

Nearby spectators muffled their laughter, and the captain grinned in the glow of Madame d'Avery's certain embarrassment. Yet the flush to her cheeks was not from embarrassment but anger.

"I can make my own way, I assure you," she said, shrugging off fleshy hands. "And you can chug away knowing I will get to the truth."

"Definitely too much seawater," laughed an admirer of the captain. Edgarton continued shaking hands with his delighted guests. He only scowled a moment when he saw a large black bird circling a fluffy white cloud.

Madame d'Avery saw the crow, too, high overhead. She couldn't help speaking aloud, as if to herself.

"Whisper, strange crow. What do you know? Can you tell me the fate of Annabel Lee?"

Back in his chambers, the captain poured himself a brandy. He poured another and awaited his dinner, as was customary on days when he rested by the shore. He stood, walked over to open the window, and returned to his desk. He closed his eyes, listening to the sounds of the land: clanging hooves, chiming church bells, the stevedores' yells, and then an all too familiar cackle: "Annabel Lee."

Edgarton opened his eyes and met the stark stare of the crow standing steadfast before him. The creature shone fiercely purple in the straight rays of the setting sun shooting through the window. Its beak gleamed gold, and it held a silver key in one clawed foot.

"Annabel Lee!" it pronounced loud and clear. It tapped its foot without the key upon the captain's red cherry desk. "Annabel Lee," it prodded impatiently.

"Dratted vermin! Be out! Be out!" Edgarton spilled his bottle of brandy in his haste to jump up from his large leather chair. He swung wildly at the crow, but it escaped out the window, cawing, "Annabel Lee!"

The captain sent for a cleaning automaton to deal with the brandy-covered desk. He opened a new bottle and, this time didn't bother pouring a drink but rather chugged it straight from the source. Sweat poured down his blotchy face, and he took his jacket off. He sat back down in his chair and felt his heart maintain its incessant racing.

Finally, after a multitude of gulps from the brandy bottle, his eyes grew foggy, as did his mind. He stumbled to his bed without supper.

A great thwacking whacking sound awakened him. He swung his thick legs over the bed and placed his stockinged feet up on the crimson-swirled Oriental rug. *Thwack! Whack!*

He rubbed his sleep-sandy eyes with meaty fists. "What in tarnation?"

Thwack! Whack!

He followed the sounds to the adjoining room: Annabel's chamber.

Thwack! Whack!

The crow was hurtling itself against the window.

"Get away, you locust!"

"Annabel Lee," the crow called out. "Annabel Lee!" Its talons clutched the silver key.

Edgarton's angry eyes widened, and his breath hitched with the shock of recognition. He knew what lock that key went to. He spun around the room as if he expected someone else to be there.

Thwack! Whack!

"Annabel Lee!"

The captain ran from the room and back to his own. Opening the top right desk drawer, he removed a revolver. Loaded and cocked, it felt light in his hand as he swung the door to the deck open. He turned the corner and shot three times.

Bam! Bam! Bam!

But there was no bird there.

"Dag nabbit," the captain cursed. He paced the deck, pursuing a bird that was no longer there. The sun dipped behind the city, and the captain returned to his chambers.

At three in the morning, a shrill scraping sound awoke him. He lit a candle and searched the room. Then he realized where the sound was coming from. Bile rose in his throat.

Slowly he opened the door to Annabel's room. Just a crack. Just enough for him to peek through. He peered in by the dim light of the candle in his hand and spied a black eye looking back at him.

"Criminy!" he swore, throwing open the door fully and bounding in.

The crow was scratching the silver key across the surface of the hope chest. Its eyes caught the fire of the lone candle and seemed to burn from within.

"What do you want?" asked the captain, his voice a cracking whisper.

"Annabel Lee!"

The captain started shaking, not in frustration, but in fright. The crow continued scraping the key against the hope chest until it found its target.

"No!" the captain cried out, falling to his knees.

But the crow did not stop. It cocked its head sideways. In its clenched beak, the silver key turned, clicked, and released the lock.

A stench like low tide filled the room.

"Now you've done it," the captain moaned. He stood and stepped forward. One step closer, two steps closer. The crow fluttered out of reach to the vanity mirror. Edgarton ignored it and stood before the popped-open hope chest as if in a trance.

"Perhaps this is a nightmare," he whispered. But he knew it was not.

He set the candle down on the low table beside him. He reached forward. His fingertips grasped the lid of the hope chest. He pulled it open slowly, carefully, and the maggoty scent enveloped him.

Finally, the lid was all the way open. Edgarton looked down. There was the body of Annabel Lee, just as he had left her. The crow alighted next to the candle.

"I warned her," the captain whimpered. "I told her next time would be the last time. She knew what would happen."

The crow's eyes glowed like hot coals and stared into his.

"What do you want of me?" came the captain's plea. "It is too late to save her, your Annabel Lee."

The crow tapped its long-toed feet upon the smooth tabletop.

"Stay away, oh wicked creature!"

The crow stared intently into the captain's eyes once more, then met the unending gaze of its mistress's corpse. Clear as a bell in the silent night, the crow opened its mouth and spoke one final time.

"Annabel Lee."

A sizzling sound filled the captain's ears. A veil of white smoke covered his visage. The candle flickered.

The sizzling subsided, and the smoke cleared. Edgarton's mouth opened in soundless horror. Sweat poured into his wide eyes.

Before him hovered the white ghostly form of his fiancée. She looked upon him but breathed not a word. The crow remained quiet.

Together, Annabel Lee and the crow drifted out the window.

When the cabin boy found him in the morning, the captain's body was squished into the strong hope chest. In his mouth lay a silver key.

❖

Annabel Lee
And the silver key
Lurching, emerging,
Deep in the sea

The Moon's Price

Doc Coleman

Sir Edmund Newington pushed himself up out of the mud. His head ached. He looked around for his rifle for a few seconds before he realized that it must still be in the holster on his saddle. He climbed back to his feet, shaking his sleeves to cast off the dirt and mud clinging to them. He brushed more dirt from his coat and the silver gorget around his neck. He tugged on his left gauntlet to make sure it was properly seated on his hand as he looked for a sign of his mount. The forest around him was dark and thick and quiet. "Damned panto," Edmund muttered to himself.

He pulled the gauntlet off his right hand and pressed it to his forehead, and it came away stained with blood. Edmund sighed. He never should have let Lord Morton talk him into coming up to Scotland for this little "hunt."

Lord Wendell Morton was always looking for some kind of favor, and it never turned out well for Edmund. This time the story was some beast attacking his herds. Wolves, probably, or a hungry bear fresh from hibernation. Lord Morton claimed it was driving him to ruin, and that it only came out of Glentress Forest at night. He'd arranged a night hunt, to lure the animal out and bring it down.

Edmund should have known better than to agree.

He should have turned back at the first sign of trouble. When the dogs had refused to go into the field, and the horses refused to come out of their stalls, Edmund should have joined them and stayed behind.

But Lord Morton pulled out several pantos and convinced him to continue with the hunt.

Pantos were the latest show of conspicuous wealth among the nobles. Mechanical horses that moved and acted like real ones. They were marvels of technology, with precision clockworks and hydraulics that were almost soundless. The first models were gleaming marvels that you couldn't put a saddle on as it would slip right off of the polished metal plates. They solved this problem by gluing real leather to the outer body, and leaving excess material to cover the joints. The end effect made it look more like a pantomime horse than a real one, and they were quickly nicknamed "pantos."

The hunters on their pantos had spread out into a line and entered the forest at a walk. He'd soon lost sight of the others, although he could hear them pushing through the brush.

Then the screams started.

The first scream sounded like Sir Oliver. It was a high-pitched, terrified scream that suddenly cut off. More noises filled the night as the other hunters reacted to his cries. Edmund tried to bring his mount around to come to the injured man's aid, but the clockwork horse turned past where he wanted. Edmund shifted his weight to maneuver the panto back, but something hit the mount from behind and it leapt immediately into a full gallop. He leaned down over the neck of the animal, unable to see in the darkness.

Branches whipped at Edmund's sides as the out-of-control machine ran through bush and copse. He tucked his face in next to his mount's body to keep his eyes from being lashed, as branches scraped over his helmet. He tried to peek over its neck to see where they were going, but another thicket made him duck back down as the branches clawed at his hunting coat.

Edmund needed to regain control of the machine quickly. He pulled back on the reins, trying to slow the panto's trajectory. As the machine's gait changed, Edmund sat up a bit…

And then he found himself waking up face down in the mud.

He had no idea how long he lay in the mud before regaining consciousness. He could barely see by the starlight that filtered down through the branches. The forest wasn't familiar, but if he could find a clearing, he might be able to locate north, and plot a course back to civilization.

He spotted a trail of flattened vegetation as he pulled his gauntlet back on, and walked back along it. After a few feet he found his helmet sitting near the base of a broken sapling. The helmet had a sizable dent on one side, and the sapling looked to have been recently snapped by a heavy blow.

A few feet away he discovered the wreckage of his panto embedded in the trunk of a large tree. Edmund rushed over to it. The mechanical horse had run straight into the trunk, which thankfully curved to one side just above where the panto hit, letting Edmund be thrown over it instead of smashing his brains out.

The body of the panto had folded up on itself, crushed against the tree. Edmund grabbed at the rifle still in the holster on the saddle. It was tightly wedged in and he had to work it back and forth to get it free.

He held up the carbine, and looked at the bend in the barrel just past the stock.

Edmund dropped the useless carbine to the ground. He wished he still had the lightning rifle he'd carried as a lieutenant in the Eternal Empress' Imperial Infantry. "May she live forever," he whispered out of reflex as the thought of the British Empress crossed his mind. With a lightning rifle, he'd be out of this in an hour or two. Just find a patch of open ground and fire bolts into the sky until the search party found him.

But the act of heroism that earned Edmund his knighthood had also cost him his left hand, and his commission in the Empress' service. The clockwork prosthetic he now wore worked well, but not well enough for Victoria's army. And they don't let civilians have lightning rifles…

Edmund tugged on his left gauntlet, making sure it was properly seated.

He looked at the back of the panto, and found that the leather on one side had been ripped away. In addition, there were five slashes in the cover plates. As if it had been attacked by Lord Morton's beast. The automaton should have gone down right away. Somehow the damage to the mechanism sent the mount into full gallop instead. That might have been the only thing that saved Edmund's life.

He looked around warily. He wasn't the only hunter in these woods tonight.

Edmund noticed a brighter section of wood off to one side. He hoped it was a clearing. At the very least, a little moonlight would make for easier going. Edmund quickened his pace and headed for the glimpse of moonlight. He tried to walk a straight path toward it, but was forced to detour frequently. The light shone bright and strong, cutting a path through the trees, like a beacon on a foggy night. He pushed through the bracken, eager to find the clearing and get his bearings. Or a stream he could follow to a town or a farm.

The moonlight he followed faded suddenly. Edmund stood still for a minute, hoping it was only obscured by a cloud, but the light didn't reappear. Finally, he continued on, projecting his path from where he last remembered seeing the light.

A tree root caught Edmund's foot, sending him crashing to the ground again. As he landed, he heard the loud boom of a shotgun, and a nearby tree exploded in fragments of bark as the pellets drove into the trunk.

"Don't shoot!" Edmund cried from his prone position on the forest floor. "I mean you no harm!"

A voice grumbled in answer. Edmund could hear mechanical sounds in the night. Like a fresh shotgun shell being loaded.

"Then you best shove off back where you came from and stop lurking about my property!" The voice brooked no argument.

"I'm doing just that," Edmund replied. "I got separated from Lord Morton's hunting party. I'm lost. I would appreciate it if you could provide me shelter for the night and help me find my way back to Lord Morton's estate in the morning."

The man grumbled. "Very well. If I don't, you'll probably wander in circles and end up right back here. I'll give you a place to sleep, and show you the road to the village in the morning. From there, you're on your own."

"Thank you." Edmund climbed to his feet cautiously, and the man stepped out of the shadows. He was tall, six foot or more, and muscular. His tattered pants and jacket had seen plenty of wear and repair over the years. A thick, dark beard covered his chin and matched the wild hair atop his head. He carried a shotgun in his meaty right hand. The weapon was pointed at the ground, but the man held it ready to quickly bring it to bear at need.

The man motioned Edmund to him. "Just mind you keep your hands to yourself, and we won't have no trouble. Come on."

"Thank you. I'm Sir Edmund Newington. And you are?"

The man snorted. "Angus will do. Don't you know better than to hunt in the woods at night, Mr. Newington?" He gestured for Edmund to precede him, indicating a path that was little more than a deer track.

Edmund walked down the narrow trail. "Lord Morton brought us up here from London. He claimed some beast was savaging his cattle. Insisted we had to hunt it at night as that was when it came out."

"Did he say what kind of animal he thought it was?" Angus asked with a wary tone.

Edmund shook his head. "No. I'm not sure that he had any idea himself. But there's something in these woods. It attacked our party…" Edmund's words cut off abruptly as the woodman struck him in the back of the head with the butt of his shotgun. The world went to black as Sir Edmund's limp body collapsed to the ground.

His head pounded as Edmund became aware of his surroundings again. He heard the muffled sound of Angus' voice as he argued loudly with someone else. He couldn't make out the other person's voice, but he heard a raven or crow in the next room, cawing out its distress at Angus' shouting. Edmund blinked open his eyes to find himself in a small room. Light leaked in around the edges of a closed door. Glancing around, he was able to make out a table and a bed. It seemed to be a bedroom in a cottage.

Edmund tried to rub the pain at the back of his head, but his hand wouldn't move from his side. It was then he realized that he was tied to a chair in the small room. He pulled against the ropes, but he was bound tight.

Angus roared in the next room, his protestations met by the caws of the crow. Edmund couldn't understand a word of the man's raging, although he was quite loud enough. He thought the man might be cursing in Gaelic at whomever he quarreled with. From the timing of the bird's croaking, it almost sounded as if his row was with the crow. Angus made one final pronouncement, and then a door slammed with enough force to make the whole cottage shake.

After the sudden noise, the cottage fell silent. Edmund sat and listened, but he heard no sound from the crow, or anyone else in the room beyond the door. He hoped that meant they left with Angus, and he would have a chance to escape.

He squirmed in his bonds, trying to find enough slack to slip them off, or reach one of the knots and work it free. He struggled for a while, trying to find some advantage that might grant him freedom before the large woodsman returned.

He barely heard the sound of someone moving in the room outside. He paused in his attempts to escape for a second, and the door opened. A woman entered holding a candle. The light seemed very bright to his eyes after growing accustomed to the dark. He winced and looked away, then looked back and nearly averted his gaze again. The woman wore only a coarse, homespun shift. It perched on her shoulders, and was closed modestly in the front, but the fabric did little to obscure her form. She was short, perhaps five feet in height, with long dark hair streaming down over her shoulders.

In her other hand, she carried a bowl with a plate stacked on top of it. "Well, I see you've rejoined us. I hope you aren't too worse for wear," she said as she elbowed the door closed and moved to the small table, setting the candle down, and then separating the bowl and plate. "I'm afraid I'm going to have to apologize for my husband. Angus means well, but he gets very over-protective when anyone comes near our home. I'm sorry that he's treated you so roughly. My name is Helen. I hope you can forgive us for the poor hospitality we've shown you thus far."

She reached into the bowl and pulled out a wet cloth, squeezing the excess water out of it. "Let me get you cleaned up a little." She sat on the edge of the bed and dabbed at Edmund's face with the damp cloth. The water was warm, but her fingers where she touched him were strangely cold. After a few swipes with the cloth, it began to show red streaks. "You've got a nasty gash on your forehead, sir. Did my Angus do that to you?" She sounded more like a concerned mother than a kidnapper's accomplice.

"No," Edmund replied before he realized what he was doing. "That was from hitting a tree. Your husband struck me on the back of the head."

"Oh, did he?" she said, and leaned Edmund's head forward while she gently probed her fingers through his hair. He hissed involuntarily when she prodded the sore spot where Angus had struck him. "Oh, sorry." She felt around more gently. Her cold fingers felt somehow comforting, and her touch helped dull the pain. "I'm afraid that you'll have a bit of a bump for a few days, but you should be just fine after that. I'll see if I can make a bandage for that gash, but I'm glad to say that you don't seem to have any serious damage."

"Am I going to live long enough for that to matter?" Edmund asked.

Helen looked at him, shock on her face. "What? Why wouldn't you?"

"I seem to be tied to a chair in your home, madam, after your husband struck me from behind. You do see how this might give a man pause about the nature of his prospects for the future." Edmund looked at her pointedly. "Why have you taken me prisoner?"

A look of sadness crossed her face. "I'm sorry. Angus insisted. He… He's been hurt in the past, and he doesn't trust strangers. That's why we moved to the woods. When someone turns up unexpectedly, he gets even more suspicious." She laid a hand down on Edmund's arm, and the rope binding him to the chair. "I'm very sorry about this, but I'm sure in the morning I can convince him that you're no danger to us. He's not a bad man, really."

"It would help if you could untie the ropes," Edmund said. "I swear by the Eternal Empress that I have no desire to hurt you. I only asked for shelter for the night. I was lost in the woods when your husband found me."

Helen reached for the plate on the table. "I would untie you, but I'm afraid that will only upset Angus more when he comes back. He wasn't in the best of moods when he left. When he returns, I'll try to get him to release you." She picked up a slice of cheese and held it up to him. "I thought you might be hungry. Would you care for some cheese? Apple slices?"

"Where did your husband go, if it is the middle of the night?" Edmund asked after swallowing a bite of cheese.

"He wanted to make sure that there wasn't anyone else near the cabin. He should be back soon. In fact, I should go out and wait for him." She stood and stacked up the plate and the bowl of water again.

"Isn't he afraid of the beast?"

She dropped the bowl and plate on the table, spilling out water onto the surface. She hastily straightened them again, then looked at Edmund. "The what?"

"The beast Lord Morton brought us out here to hunt. Morton claimed it had been killing his cattle. I'm fairly certain that it injured or killed more than one of our hunting party."

"Oh, no. Did you use that word with Angus?"

"Um… I think I did. Right before he hit me on the back of the head."

A loud *thump* came from the outer room; like a door being opened with force and hitting furniture, or perhaps the wall. Helen jumped at the noise.

"HELEN!" Angus' voice filled the small cottage.

She dropped the dishes on the table. Padding quietly over to the door to the outer room, she peeked out. Helen closed the door again, and looked around the room. Rushing to the window, she partially opened the sash but hesitated again. Finally making up her mind, she moved over between the bed and Edmund and positioned herself behind his chair.

"Please," she said, "Don't let Angus know that I was here. He'll just jump to all the wrong conclusions."

"What?" Edmund said, but the woman paid no attention to him. She squatted down behind him and began chanting something in a low voice. As best he could make it out it was "Cailleach thoir dhomh do chumhachd." With each repetition of the phrase her voice became rougher and hoarser until it was barely a croak. As she repeated the words, the light in the room also seemed to dim, as if the brightness was being pulled back into the candle.

With a croaking caw, a crow jumped up onto Edmund's shoulder. It perched there for a moment, its cold claws digging into his stained coat and chilling his flesh. The bird cocked its head, looking at him with one eye and giving a short chuff, before launching itself into the air, and flying out the open window.

Edmund stared after the creature for a moment, then turned to look at Helen, hiding behind him. Not seeing her, he twisted in his chair, turning it slightly with a loud squeak of wood against the floor, but the woman was gone. Her shift lay in a pile on the floor, but of her, there was no sign.

"HELEN!" Angus called again from the outer room. Edmund shifted back toward the door. He wished he could wake up, safe in his bed in London, making this whole experience a bad dream.

The door flung open, and Angus stepped in, filling the opening. The man seemed somehow bigger than before. His jacket and shirt were gone, exposing a chest covered with thick hair over a network of old scars. Dirt caked his pants, and Edmund noticed splatters of fresh blood as well.

The woodsman looked down at the table, where the candle still burned, and the two dishes revealed that his captive had not been alone. Edmund looked up at the man's face just as Angus strode across the small room and grabbed him by the chin. The woodsman's large hand gripped his face like a vise.

"Where is she? What have you been doing with her?" the larger man growled and Edmund felt like he was trying to pick him up, chair and all.

"I don't know where she is! I don't know what is going on. I swear by the Eternal Empress, I did nothing to her! She came in and looked at my wounds, that's it. Please, sir, I just want to go home. I can pay you ransom. I have silver. You'll never hear from me again, I promise you!"

Angus growled deep in his chest again, sounding more like an animal than a man. He raised his other hand up, as if to strike Edmund, when the crow flew back into the room. It circled around the larger man's head, cawing loudly and battering his face with its wings.

The woodsman stepped back and put his hands up to defend his face. "Helen!" he cried, "stop this! What do you think you're up to, witch? You know what has to be done. They were hunting us. We can't leave any of them. They'll just come back with more. You heard him threaten me with silver. Let me end this quickly." The crow cawed loudly, as if shouting at him. It swooped at him again and again, and managed to get past his defenses and place a long scratch on his cheek with one of its talons.

He howled in pain, and the crow backed off a bit. Edmund stared in shock as the wound, red, bloody, and angry, closed in front of his eyes. Angus shook his head, and the blood flung from his cheek, leaving it clean and unblemished.

"Enough, Helen!" Angus yelled. "This has to be done."

He stepped toward Edmund once more, and the crow dove at him, but the woodsman expected it this time. He scooped the bird out of the air and tossed it across the room. It hit the wall and collapsed into a pile of feathers that quickly slid behind the headboard of the bed.

"Did you think to take this one for a lover, Helen?" Angus pulled a knife from his belt. "Well, I can quickly take care of that." He advanced on Edmund again.

Light burst from behind the bed, startling Edmund and momentarily blinding Angus. A feathered arm reached up onto the bed, black feathers falling away to reveal milky white skin below. The hand grabbed the bedclothes, and Helen pulled herself up from the floor. Inky feathers fell away from her body, revealing her completely naked form, glowing with an impossible inner light. "Angus, no!" she cried.

Her husband reared back, howling in agony. The hair on his chest thickened, spreading up his neck and down his arms like wildfire, leaving fur instead of ash in its wake. He cried out again and fell to the ground, as Edmund heard the crack of bones. When Angus raised his head, his face had been stretched out into the muzzle of a wolf. Shadows danced against the wall behind him, cast by the light coming from Helen's skin. They twisted as the man transformed, casting off the seeming of a man to become a gigantic wolf.

The knife clattered across the floorboards, and Angus' pants fell from him, as his wolf body became too narrow for the belt to hold them up. His legs bent backward as he stomped on the fabric with his paws. The wolf growled as it faced Edmund.

Desperate to be free of his bonds, Edmund twisted his body, drawing the ropes tight about him, then flexed the muscles in his left arm just so… and his mechanical hand detached with a slight pop. Edmund pulled his stump through the coils of rope, giving him the slack he needed to free his other hand and begin disentangling himself from his bonds. As the ropes went slack, his prosthetic hand fell to the floor.

Helen called to her husband, "Angus, get out! Out of the house! Don't do this!"

Ignoring her, he leapt forward, falling on Edmund and lunging for his neck. The chair shattered beneath them as the giant wolf attacked, snapping the wooden legs and arms and driving Edmund to the ground. The creature opened its massive jaws and bit him. Edmund cried out as the creature's teeth drove through the layers of his wool hunting coat, vest, and shirt and into his shoulder in the back, while the teeth of the jaw drove into the gorget that still hung around Edmund's neck. The chain that held it in place snapped as the creature yelped and pulled back, ripping the piece of armor away.

Angus' teeth had driven into the piece of metal. It whined in pain and shook its head to free itself from the silver piece. Wisps of smoke climbed from its mouth.

Wincing through his own pain, Edmund pushed himself upright and finished freeing himself from the ropes and debris that was left of the chair. Helen grabbed a blanket from the bed with one hand and used it to cover herself, but she gestured with her other hand. "Angus! Go! Go! Now!"

Edmund pulled his sleeve up and hastily re-fitted his clockwork arm. He flexed, to test the connection, and the fingers of his left hand wiggled in response. Reflexively, he tugged the gauntlet up.

With another shake of his head, Angus sent the dented gorget flying across the room to bounce against the wall.

Helen stepped toward him. "Please, Angus, go!"

The wolf looked to her, then to Edmund, and lunged again. Edmund threw his left arm up in defense. He felt the hot, wet gust of the animal's breath as it spread its jaws wide. It dug its teeth into the leather gauntlet and thrashed its head to rend the flesh, but try as it might, Edmund's prosthetic arm withstood the attack.

While his arm remained undamaged, Edmund was shaken thoroughly. In a flash of insight, he realized why the tiny gorget had such an effect on the creature. *Of course, it's silver! Silver is supposed to hurt werewolves.* But now the ceremonial piece of armor was across the room, out of reach.

Edmund balled his right hand into a fist and struck Angus hard on the tip of his nose. This had the desired effect, making the wolf release his grip on Edmund's arm and take a step back. Edmund grabbed the fingers of his left-hand gauntlet and yanked hard, pulling the stained leather glove off the smooth metal fingers beneath. Then he lunged at Angus, his gleaming silver fingers widespread, and grabbed his muzzle, which immediately began to smoke.

Surprised, the wolf pulled back, desperate to avoid another touch from the metal. Edmund scrambled after the beast, reaching with his mechanical hand, and forcing the monstrous animal to retreat before him. He continued to beat back the wolf until it ran out the door of the room to get away from the burning metal.

Edmund slammed the door closed, and leaned his back against it, panting heavily.

Helen stood up from the bed, the blanket clutched to her and came over to kneel next to Edmund. "Did he bite you?"

Edmund stared at her. "Did he bite me? Madam, your husband is a werewolf, and all you can think to ask is 'Did he bite you?'"

She gave Edmund a pitying look. "Yes. He's a werewolf, and you have a silver hand for some reason. I am a moon witch. The light of the moon shines through me at night. I'm a healer, but I can't cure his curse. We can only be together when I take the form of the Cailleach, the Raven. It's not an easy life, but it is the life we share." She reached forward and touched Edmund's shoulder. He flinched, and she pulled her hand back. A smear of blood shone brightly on the pale skin of her hand. She sighed. "I'm so sorry, I wanted him to let you go. I didn't think you knew enough to cause us problems. But now we don't have a choice anymore."

Edmund gave her a wary look. "What? What do you mean by that? What are you going to do?"

Her eyes brimmed with tears as she stood and took two steps back from him. "I'm not going to do anything. The silver will."

"The doctor said they use silver to prevent infection," he replied, then gasped and grabbed at his arm. He cried out in pain. "What did you do?" A burning sensation crept up his arm. It was worst where the metal of the prosthetic met his flesh. He gritted his teeth as his arm erupted with pain, but he could only bear it for a few moments. Edmund flexed the muscles in his arm, causing the prosthetic to detach. He grabbed it and tossed it away from him, but the agony continued.

Helen shook her head, dislodging tears from her eyes. "I'm so sorry," she said. "You didn't deserve any of this."

Edmund looked at her, not understanding her words as his fingers dug at the end of his stump, and the silver ring that joined the prosthetic to his body. A surge of pain went through him, and he doubled forward on the floor.

"I'm afraid there's nothing I can do to help," Helen said.

Another surge of agony came, and Edmund sprawled face down on the floor. He heard a large crack, as his bones began to break and re-shape. He looked down at his right hand as fur pushed out through his skin, and his fingers twisted into hard, sharp claws. He tried to speak, to ask why this was happening to him, but all that came out was a whine. He felt his cheeks snap and reform as his nose stretched out, and his ears moved up and back on his head. A sudden flood of scents overwhelmed him, most notable among them fear, smoke, and a scent he recognized as himself. His body convulsed and stretched and his clothes were either tight or loose. Buttons popped, fabric tore, and slid along his fur as he dug at his left sleeve, trying to get rid of the souce of the torment.

His claws tore through the thick wool of his hunting jacket, and the shirt beneath it, exposing the metal band that anchored his replacement arm. The skin around the band smoked and bubbled as if the metal was red hot. Edmund swiped at it again with his claws, before instinct took over and he started biting at his stump with his powerful jaws. He whined and growled as he struggled to remove the fitting, while his body spasmed with waves of pain, and the effects of his first change. Blood sprayed across the floor as his teeth dug into his flesh, desperate to stop the agony. The torture grew, and Edmund became more frantic as his strength flowed out of him. His growls turned into piteous whines, and his struggles became a faint scrabbling to flee the danger embedded in his flesh.

In the end, the wolf lay still on the floor of the small cottage. The last light faded from his eyes, and the fresh pelt of fur slowly withdrew back into his skin. The muzzle pulled back from the savaged arm, and took on human features again. The man the world knew as Sir Edmund Newington lay on the floor, dead, lying in a pool of his own blood.

"I'm so sorry," Helen said.

The Day Baltimore Burned

A Story in the Clockwork Chronicles Universe

Michelle D. Sonnier

Saturday, February 6, 1904

ROSALIE DOTEN SPUN A SLOW CIRCLE IN THE GRACIOUSLY appointed front hall of a posh row house on Lee Street in the Otterbein neighborhood of Baltimore. It wasn't the first time she'd delivered her work to the genteel homes of captains of industry in this German neighborhood. She hoped it would not be the last because the daughters and wives here paid well to use her wares. Rosalie fingered the silken handkerchief that held one of her Secret Sparrows. A little brass bird that fit neatly in the palm of a lady's hand, with a secret compartment in its belly that allowed lovers to send messages and small tokens of affection privately. She also made little clockwork orioles that would sing whatever pretty little tune the customer asked her to magic in. Certain ladies liked those better, but the Secret Sparrows were, without doubt, her best seller.

Of all the times she'd gone through this particular type of transaction, this one stood out. That someone who'd purchased one of her birds was willing to spend what Rosalie considered a ridiculous amount of money to ensure her silence was not unusual. That kind of transaction was her bread and butter, keeping a roof over her head and food in her belly. The odd thing about this purchase was the whos and the hows. Usually, both members of the couple would manage a discrete rendezvous with her so she could imprint the bird with their identities at the same time. Sometimes a young, or not-so-young, miss would buy one and ask that it be delivered to a man, where Rosalie would perform the second imprint. She wondered how many of those little sparrows made it back to the lady who purchased them. Or did they languish on a shelf or in a drawer somewhere? Gathering dust, their message of affection unread… Rosalie shook her head to clear it.

A gentleman purchased this one. He arranged to meet her in Druid Hill Park. Something about him made Rosalie's stomach flip when she first laid eyes on him. He wore expensive, well-cared-for clothing of the latest fashion. But his hygiene did not match his attire. His hair hung greasy and lank, his beard untrimmed, and a certain odor wafted off him, telling Rosalie that he didn't avail himself of regular bathing. The rounded slump of his back indicated either bad posture or an unfortunately formed spine. None of that on its own would have bothered Rosalie. She'd been born in the gutters of Baltimore, near the docks, of a desperate mother and an unknown father. She knew a disagreeable visage could house a generous soul full of compassion and loyalty. But his eyes… Something about his eyes sent shivers down Rosalie's spine. She'd seen butchers regard cows with more kindness and respect before taking a sledgehammer to their foreheads to kill them.

Footsteps pattered on the stairs behind her. She turned to see another lovely and spoiled young miss descending with an impish smile upon her lips. She paused to look Rosalie up and down, taking in her mannish dress of trousers, a thick overcoat, and a flat cap with her hair tucked beneath. Rosalie found that she could make her way around the city with much less interference if people easily mistook her for a young boy rather than a young woman.

"Miss Doten? So pleased to make your acquaintance." She clasped her hands in front of her and bobbed a little with excitement. "Clara told me you have something for me?"

Rosalie smiled. "As long as you are Charlotte Meier, I certainly do."

"Of course I am." Charlotte extended her hand imperiously. "Are you expecting additional funds?"

"No, Miss Meier, the gentleman has already paid in full. He only asked that I be sure to deliver it to you and only you and that you open it in private."

Charlotte's eye twinkled. "In private? Give it to me!"

Rosalie deposited the silk-wrapped bundle into the girl's hand, touched the brim of her flat cap, and turned to go. Charlotte called out to her.

"Miss Doten?"

Rosalie paused and turned to see Charlotte frowning at the initials embroidered in the corner of the silk handkerchief knotted around the Secret Sparrow.

"Is this handkerchief one you supplied?" Miss Meier asked.

"No, miss. It's from the gentleman himself. He insisted on loading the bird out of my sight, and when he brought it back, it was wrapped in that handkerchief."

The rich, young miss puzzled over the embroidered letters. "Who sent it?"

"He did not give me a name, and I did not ask," Rosalie responded. "The discretion I offer is more easily accomplished when I don't even know myself."

Charlotte narrowed her eyes. "What did he look like? Tall? Fair?"

It occurred to Rosalie that this Secret Sparrow didn't come from the admirer Charlotte expected. Rosalie grinned at her and said, "He was average height and dark-haired. It would seem you have an embarrassment of riches." Rosalie touched the brim of her cap again and skipped out the door.

Trotting down Exeter Street, Rosalie patted the bag at her side. With her deliveries done for the day, it was time to go show Kory her latest invention. Working on the new project had been a welcome reprieve from spelling Secret Sparrows.

The original spellwork and design she based Secret Sparrows on had been worked out by the technomancer who started it all, Arabella Helene Leyden, back on the shores of merry old England. But Rosalie had made a few refinements. To begin with, her technique for tuning it between two lovers was much cleaner and more elegant than the original, and the birds themselves more delicate and compact. She'd submitted it to the American Witches Council to register Secret Sparrows as her work. Any other witch performing her registered work would be required to remit a fee to Rosalie. Rosalie grinned at the thought of not having to be the one at the beck and call of snooty rich folk but still getting to collect a cut. She'd have money to live off and more time to follow her dreams. But the Council hadn't gotten back to her yet. It had been months… bloody bureaucracy. While she waited for them to tell her that the spell was hers and she could charge a royalty, another witch could be copy-catting her right now, which would throw doubt on her claim and force her to endure months more of forms and interviews and waiting.

Rosalie caught sight of Gunner's Hall, where Kory worked as a bartender, and put all thoughts of bureaucracy out of her mind. Just as she crossed the street, Rosalie heard a caw. The air stirred above her head, and a crow landed on her shoulder.

"Hello, Ryan." Rosalie laughed. "Do you want to visit Kory too?" Ryan cawed and bobbed his head.

As Rosalie stepped into Gunner's Hall, the heat enveloped her right away, working to thaw her out from her long walk in the early February air. Ryan remained on her shoulder until she shed her wool overcoat and climbed onto a stool at the end of the bar. The big crow flapped once to reach the bar. He hopped and cawed to get the attention of the barman on duty, a dear friend to Rosalie and himself, Kory. Rosalie leaned back on the stool, propping her back on the wall, enjoying further thawing. She knew Ryan would let Kory know what they wanted.

Kory Kaese looked up from wiping the bar and smiled. He kept his sandy hair short, but his mustache was luxurious in the fashion of the time. His white shirt and apron were immaculate. A bit of his daring bright blue waistcoat peeped out from behind the apron. Those who did not know Kory might think him just another broad-shouldered barman hired more for his ability to clear out a rowdy crowd. He could indeed clear a rowdy crowd when the need arose, but those who knew Kory knew the gentle, intelligent soul on the inside. Rosalie loved to talk to him about her latest work. He frequently helped her talk it out when one element or another had her stuck. Ryan liked that Kory gave him roasted peanuts in the shell and didn't complain when he had to clean up after the crow.

Bright blue eyes twinkling, Kory brought the witch and the crow their usual order. A hard cider for the lady, and peanuts and a shallow dish of fresh water for the feathered gentleman.

"You look like you're having a good day," Kory said as he brushed Ryan's first peanut shell into a small tin bucket.

"Better than a day, and better than good," said Rosalie with a grin. She took a long pull on her cider. "Ah, the best cider in all of Baltimore."

"You've gone to other bars and sampled their wares?" Kory put his hand to his forehead in mock dismay. "I thought you kept your thirst only for me."

"Well, there are some nights you don't work…." Rosalie said with a wink.

Kory laughed and flipped more peanut shells into the bucket. "What makes this week so special?"

"Good sales to start. I'll eat well for a while. But I also had time to figure a few things out…" Rosalie patted the canvas bag in her lap.

Standing more alert at her words, Ryan strutted up and down the bar. He flared his wings and presented his talons, twisting his head from side to side. Rosalie laughed at his antics.

"I don't need you to model for this one."

Ryan clacked his beak at her in a huff. He returned to his peanuts with a vengeance.

"You're a wonderful model, my dear," Rosalie crooned as she petted his head with one finger. "But you're not shaped like a spyglass."

Ryan ruffled his feathers, then offered his head to Rosalie for more pets.

"You figured out the spyglass, then?" Kory asked.

"Indeed," Rosalie said. She placed a burnished brass spyglass on the bar with gentle fingers.

Kory regarded it for a moment. "It looks very… normal."

Rosalie cocked her head to the side. "Perhaps I should do something to the casing to distinguish it from a regular spyglass."

"But you solved the problem?"

Rosalie nodded. "The trick was spelling the tiny mirrors to shift independently to gather enough moonlight and starshine to see. I got the idea after watching flowers follow the sun to catch as much light as they can all day."

"So a man could look through this in the dead of night and see what's in the distance clear as day?" Kory asked.

Rosalie nudged his elbow where it rested on the bar. "Or a woman…"

"Or a woman." Kory chuckled.

"But yes, that's exactly what it does," Rosalie said. "I think sailors will be very interested in them. Imagine the watch being able to spot hazards or crew overboard in the middle of the night. This could mean something… It could save lives."

Kory nodded. "I bet you could make hefty sales to soldiers as well. Make it a lot easier to spy on the enemy…"

Rosalie frowned. "And easier to shoot the men just going about their business in the middle of the night. I'm not interested in selling to soldiers. We've had too much war."

Kory patted her hand. "I know you won't sell them to soldiers, but once you register your spell with the Council, what's to stop another technomancer from doing it?"

"Nothing," Rosalie whispered. She drew into herself, the shine of her earlier happiness gone. Ryan worked his beak under her hand, shoving his head into her palm. Rosalie petted him absently. "Maybe I should just put it away. Pretend I never made it..."

Kory shook his head. "What about those sailors overboard? The lives it could save?"

"What about the soldiers who would use it to take lives?" Rosalie retorted.

Kory held up his hands for peace. "I don't want to argue."

"You're doing a fine job of it," Rosalie snapped.

"I just want you to think things through and be prepared for any consequences," Kory soothed. "And you know just putting it away won't change things. It will just delay things. Some other technomancer will eventually get the same idea."

A patron at the other end of the bar called Kory's name. He patted Rosalie's hand. "Just think things through. Be prepared."

She did ponder the quandary as she shared Ryan's peanuts. Kory kept her glass full and tended to the other patrons. Rosalie watched Kory fondly as he held court with some fisherman in for a pint before they headed home to their wives. She came here because Kory challenged her; and even when his challenges irritated her, they were useful. She couldn't bury her head in the sand about the possible uses for her new spells and gizmos. Better to go into things with clear eyes. Her mother would have boxed her ears for trying to ignore the bad things. She said it was stupid and dangerous to do that. At least Kory only used his words to remind Rosalie to keep an eye out for hazardous possibilities.

Three ciders in, Rosalie's anger had seeped away, and she saw that Kory was right. She had to find a way to be at peace with someone else using her creations for purposes she had never thought of, or she had to know that some other witch would eventually spell something similar. Either way, she had no control over how her creation was used once it left her hands.

A blast of frigid February air drew Rosalie's attention to the door. Two cops stood just inside, surveying the room with grim gazes. The one with the florid black mustache caught sight of Rosalie, then pointed to her as he whispered in his partner's ear. The other nodded tightly. They turned sharp on their heels and marched to where she sat. As they loomed over her, Ryan clacked his beak and hissed. The cops backed up a step.

"Are you Miss Rosalie Doten?" asked the mustached cop.

"I…" Rosalie's mind was blank. Her eyes flicked to Ryan and Kory, but neither seemed to know what to do any more than she did. Her old harbor guttersnipe instincts kicked in.

"Who wants to know?"

"Me," growled the clean-shaven cop as he fingered the billy club on his belt.

"What do you want her for?" Kory asked, his voice pitched low and soothing.

The cops didn't take their eyes off Rosalie. The mustached one said, "She's wanted for the murder of Miss Charlotte Meier of Otterbein."

"What?" Rosalie burst out. "She was alive when I left her this afternoon!"

"So, you are Rosalie Doten!" He whipped his billy club off his belt and lunged for Rosalie.

Ryan flew up off the bar, diving at the policemen's faces. They shouted and tried to ward him off. Rosalie worried that one of them might clip Ryan with a billy club and harm the dear crow. But she wasn't going to waste the chance Ryan gave her.

She grabbed her coat and canvas bag and shot across the room for the front door. Glancing back as she stood in the doorway, she saw Kory had come over the bar to stand between her and the cops. Scratches covered their faces, but Ryan perched safely behind the bar on the top rail, taunting the police at the top of his voice. Secure in the knowledge that her friends could handle themselves, Rosalie disappeared into the night.

Rosalie kept to the shadows in Federal Hill Park. Once she was sure the police weren't on her heels after she ran from Gunner's Hall, she'd just kept walking. Walking to keep warm. Walking because she didn't know what else to do. She didn't dare go home. If the cops knew to find her at Gunner's Hall, it would be even easier to find out her home address. She stamped her feet and rubbed her hands together. She needed to find a place to get inside soon. People without shelter froze to death on nights like this.

A friendly caw came out of the night. Ryan ghosted to a landing on the grass in front of her.

"Oh, Ryan," Rosalie cried. She scooped him up and cuddled him to her chest. Ryan didn't squirm too much. He seemed to know his friend needed to express her relief and affection. Rosalie let him go after a moment. He climbed up her coat from her arms to her shoulder. He leaned his head down to press on her cheek. She knew what he wanted, even if it was difficult for her.

Rosalie opened her mind and communed with the crow. Some witches found this easy, but Rosalie wasn't one of them. She found herself lost in a welter of images – herself, Kory, the bar, peanuts, Kory, the cops with bloody faces finally leaving the bar and shaking their fists at Ryan… Kory. A nest. Kory.

"Kory has a place for me to stay? A safe place?" Rosalie asked. Ryan cawed once. "All I need to do is follow you?" Ryan's head bobbed up and down. Relief flooded Rosalie. But that relief was short-lived.

"I don't think you'll be going there tonight or ever," came a voice from behind her. A rough hand grabbed her by her upper arm, pulling her off balance. Ryan rose in the air, cawing in distress.

Rosalie whipped her head around. She gasped. It was the man who bought the Secret Sparrow and sent it to Charlotte Meier. Rosalie tried to yank her arm back. "What do you think you're doing?"

"Destroying evidence." The man's creepy smile made Rosalie shiver. "Can't have you telling the police who had you deliver the deadly little trinket to Miss Meier…"

Rosalie gasped. She struggled again. Her cap slipped off her head and onto the frozen ground. "You killed her, and you used me to do it."

"A female with the ability to reason! How rare… I shall be moderately disappointed to destroy you."

Rosalie stomped on his foot, using his momentary reaction to yank her arm from his grasp. But he recovered quickly. His hand shot out and grabbed a deep handful of her hair. He twisted his hand, and pain lanced through Rosalie's scalp. He yanked her head close to his mouth.

His foul breath made her gag as he said, "Ah, ah, ah. Resisting your betters is foolish and futile. You'll only wear yourself out."

Rosalie panted. She wondered where Ryan was; then she heard a rustle of twigs above her. He waited for the best time to intervene; she just had to be ready. She pushed at the man's hand and yanked at his sleeve. His grip was iron hard. He laughed at her.

"How did you find me?" she ground between clenched teeth, hoping to buy more time.

The man chuckled. "It was too simple. I just followed the police to find you in your den of iniquity. Really, what good woman frequents are bar?" he sneered. "And then when you ran like I knew you would, I followed you. To here. And then I watched you, waited for your hope to ebb, for your fear to teach you what I already knew." He yanked her hair again, making her gasp. "No woman is better than me, not even a witch."

Ryan dove, screeching out of the tree above. Rosalie kicked out and caught the man's shin but his grip on her hair remained tight. He whipped his cane around his head, trying to hit Ryan. With her head pulled back as it was, Rosalie saw that a heavy-looking silver knob topped the cane. She cried out as knob connected with Ryan. The crow fell to the ground with a heavy thud. He didn't move. It was too dark for Rosalie to see whether or not he still breathed.

"Ryan, no!" Rosalie sobbed.

"Oh, shut up!" snapped the man. He brought his cane up again, the knob aimed at Rosalie. Sharp pain exploded across the bridge of her nose, and darkness claimed her.

Rosalie woke to the press of cool stone beneath her cheek with no idea where she was. Her head pounded as if her heart had taken residence there, and she couldn't breathe through her nose. Whether it was from blood or breakage, she didn't know. Trying to move, she found her arms bound behind her and her ankles tied tight together. Trembling with the effort, she forced her swollen eyes open what little she could. Mid-morning sunlight leaked through small, square windows high up in the walls. Even that gentle light made her wince. What little area she could see around her revealed sacks of flour, barrels of pickles, and boxes of nails—she was in a storage area for a dry goods store.

"Oh, good, you're awake." His voice sent a shiver down Rosalie's spine. "I was afraid you'd miss the next part." Charlotte's murderer stepped into Rosalie's view. He rattled a box of matches in his hand. "You already missed how I got rid of that little trollop. It would be a shame to miss the final act, too."

"What did you do?" Rosalie wheezed, again stalling for time. Although she didn't know why. Her magic would not serve to untie bonds or burn them away. That was not where her talent lay. Her lack of ability at telepathy was another handicap. And how would anyone know she was here? She'd disappeared in the middle of the night. Ryan, the only creature with any idea what happened to her, was likely dead.

"Oh, it was a thing of beauty," the man said with a wistful sigh. "It took me quite some time to perfect my plan. Your twee little bird paired with a delicate glass vial full of deadly gas that would break as soon as she opened the trinket. I wish I could have seen it or at least heard it…. She probably screamed so prettily."

"You're a monster," Rosalie whispered.

"No!" he shrieked. "She was the monster! She! Was! The Monster!" Spittle flew from his lips. "She toyed with my heart. She smiled at me, led me astray. Then she laughed at me when I asked her to accompany me to the theater. She humiliated me on purpose!"

As much as his rant frightened her, Rosalie hoped he would continue screaming. If he attracted anyone's attention, there was a chance she might get out of this alive.

"Enough!" he snapped. "I'll not let you toy with me, as well." Pulling a match from the box with a wicked grin, he stooped to strike it on the stone floor. Then, with the faintest of smirks, casually dropped the match on the sack of flour next to him. The bag began to smolder. The murderer stepped out of Rosalie's vision, his footsteps scuffing against the stone. She cringed at the scrape of more matches striking again and again. Panic gripped her as the acrid scent of smoke reached her nose. Rosalie could hear the fire crackling merrily in something more flammable. Somewhere to her left, hinges squealed, and his voice called out to her. "There's a sweet young lady in North Baltimore whom I've had my eye on. Surely, she will appreciate me. Not like you trampy South Baltimore girls…"

The door slammed. Rosalie twisted and struggled against the ropes. She screamed until her voice grew hoarse, which didn't take long as the thickening layer of smoke sank closer to the floor. Desperate, she willed her bonds to unravel, but no sudden telekinetic abilities surfaced. Coughing and choking and increasingly panicked, she struggled to project her thoughts to anyone receptive, praying for a latent telepathic power to bloom. Her mind remained stubbornly devoid of any voice but her own. Tears streamed down her face.

Somewhere nearby, glass shattered.

"Help, help! I'm here," her voice crackled out in a broken whisper. A familiar caw echoed out of the smoke.

"Ryan? Ryan, is that you?"

The flutter of wings was her only answer as a familiar weight alighted on her arm. Rosalie felt his beak and talons picking at the twine on her wrists. Sweat rolled down Rosalie's face. She spread her wrists as much as she was able. Ryan continued to tear at the fibers even as she stretched and held them taut. Finally, her bonds snapped as the twine unraveled. Wracked by violent coughs, Rosalie pulled her aching body up from the floor and unbound the twine at her ankles.

Then, dropping low beneath the smoke, Rosalie crawled along the floor, coughing and gasping. Ryan hopped right next to her, guiding the way. When she reached the door, she rose up on her knees and yanked it open. The fire roared and flared overhead as frigid air rushed in, feeding it. Ducking her head, Rosalie scrambled desperately up three steps to the street level and lay gasping on the sidewalk. The sidewalk was nearly empty. It was Sunday, the only day of rest for many workers in the city. Hearing the clatter of hooves approaching, Rosalie rolled over on her back and turned her gaze to the sky. Kory scrambled down from a chestnut horse with a white blaze. A murder of crows circling over his head.

Kneeling beside her, he gently lifted her off the pavement. As he placed her on the horse he cried out "Fire!" and then mounted up behind her.

"We need to get you to a doctor," he grunted as he nudged the horse into motion. Rosalie dug her fingers into the horse's mane and held on.

"No doctor. Council House. Healing witch." Rosalie started coughing and couldn't stop. With a grimace, Kory continued to call out his warning as they galloped away. The crows streamed out behind them.

Once she caught her breath, Rosalie asked Kory, "Where did you get a horse?"

"Oh, fine," he grumbled playfully. "We rescue you, and your first thought is to hint that we're horse thieves."

"Well, I want to hear that story too. Just… I need to know if I might be dodging cops again." Rosalie tried to laugh but was overcome by another coughing fit.

"No more talking," Kory murmured by her ear, "I *borrowed* the horse from the man who delivers our beer." Rosalie could hear the concern in his voice, though he tried to sound jovial. "And he knows about it too. I'll tell you the rest once we get you better."

Kory dismounted outside the Witches Council House and gently lifted Rosalie down as Ryan and the other crows zoomed through the open transom windows, cawing all the way. Once on the ground, Rosalie and Kory looked back toward the city for the first time. A massive column of smoke rose over south Baltimore. Church bells rang an endless warning.

"Oh my God…" Kory gasped. "It's already huge. How will they be able to put it all out?"

"The witches will help," Rosalie croaked. "But there will still be considerable damage. It's already gone too far."

"That bastard… he just murders and destroys, then walks away," Kory growled.

"Maybe he won't escape the fire," Rosalie said. "But even if he does, the Guardians will be on him for what he did to me. A Guardian never loses her prey."

Ángel de la Muerte

Danielle Ackley-McPhail

ALETA ANGELINA FABRICIO KNELT BEFORE HER FAMILY'S graves for a very long time.

Long enough, the end of one day became the beginning of the next. Long enough, the murmurs of the surrounding *Día de los Muertos* celebrations faded away as families went home or lay down to rest beside their loved ones' graves. Long enough, the autumn night's chill seeped through her cotton robe and into her bones. Lina nearly tumbled away at the barest touch on her shoulder, calling her back to the dark blanket of night and the low, smoldering embers of nearly spent candles glinting throughout the graveyard like fireflies. She would have fallen if not for the thick, sturdy haft bracing her. Her grip tightened on the smooth wood handle of Santa Muerte's scythe, which had replaced the cobbled-together prop Lina had left home with.

Slowly, as if fighting to turn against thick, clinging aether, Lina glanced up over her shoulder. Her right eye burned where the thin glass lens attached to her father's spirit goggles hugged its surface. The left merely burned from spent tears, as it bore no lens. She blinked and swayed, disoriented as the fading wisps of lingering spirits wafted in plain sight, though her goggles shouldn't function without being paired with those worn by her father's crow, Beltran.

Lina bit back a sob. She had lost both father and crow in one brief slash by her own hand, their spirits freed from an unfettered evil that had possessed them.

Shuttering that fresh pain, she focused on the moment, looking up at the one standing over her, nearly too far away to touch. Lina blinked and pushed the goggles to the top of her head, removing the glass disk from her eye so she could better see.

Much in the way of the restless spirits, the gaze she met swirled with intense emotion, in this instance, a mix of anger and hurt and concern. For a moment, reality seemed to flux between the spirit and mortal realm as if Lina's prolonged use of the goggles had caused the two to overlap. Wisps of aether clung to her grandmother's features, but Lina blinked, and they faded away. Even so, something seemed off with Abuela's color.

"Abuela…"

Her grandmother frowned down at her. Then she took in the goggles perched on Lina's head, paired with the calaveras mask and faded blue cotton robe she wore in a silent plea to Santa Muerte for her blessing, and the frown deepened. Lina and her grandmother had fought earlier over her manner of dress, and Abuela's disapproval clearly had not softened. The frown turned into a scowl, and Abuela quickly shuffled away to fuss over the oferenda, though she herself had arranged the altar earlier in the day.

"You plan to stay up all night, niña?"

Niña, not mija. The surface of Lina's heart cracked like aged porcelain.

She pushed to her feet. The hand she reached out to her grandmother trembled faintly as guilt pinched her belly. Her mother's mother shrugged away before they could touch. Lina frowned as a small ache settled in her chest. Her grandmother was all she had left, yet the two of them only seemed to spark like flint to steel.

Bad enough, they had fought on this of all days, but worse, the precious moment she had deprived Abuela of through her obstinance. If not for Lina's insistence on dressing as she had, her grandmother might have come with her tonight. Might have been there to greet the spirits of her daughter—Lina's mother—and her grandson, whom neither of them had ever seen among the living; of course, if not for Papa's goggles, of which Abuela most definitely did *not* approve, perhaps neither of them would have been blessed with that sight.

Lina moved to where her grandmother stood before the oferenda. "Please, Abuela. Don't worry about that. We can take care of it tomorrow."

"Nonsense. It is shamefully in disarray."

Lina closed her mouth on her pointless argument, lips pressing in a thin line. She leaned her scythe against a nearby tree and bent to straighten up the altar as her grandmother wished before laying out their straw pallets for sleeping beside the grave, as the other families around them had already done. It would be an uncomfortable night, but it showed honor to the spirits of their loved ones to spend these precious hours in their presence before Death's shroud separated them once more, until the next year.

"The food…" Abuela called out, her voice rife with censure. "Why have you not placed the food on the oferenda? Ay, dios mios! Who will do this *properly* when I am gone?"

Frantic, Lina glanced around in the dark for her basket, dropped in the battle with the evil spirit that had stolen her father's form, whom she had vanquished with the help of Lady Death herself. Puzzled, Lina found the basket sitting nearby as if set down neatly and not dropped. As she knelt to pick it up, a gentle rustle reached her ears, along with a faint, familiar muttering she thought never to hear again.

Her breath trapped within her throat, she opened the basket and peered inside.

Satiny darkness and the faint gleam of a polished brass cowl stared back.

Gasping, Lina nearly tumbled back in shock.

Beltran. Her father's crow. His spirit's prison. Still wearing the cowl Papa had engineered to work with the goggles Lina wore, allowing the wearer to glimpse across the Veil to the spirit realm. Just hours before, Lina had cradled the crow as her scythe severed its life's bonds and set her father's soul free. And yet, that wicked beak now darted out and lightly pinched her finger as it had so often before. Lina laughed a startled laugh before raising her gaze to the heavens. She sent a prayer of thanks to Santa Muerte, for surely only she could have restored the crow. But why? For a moment, Lina would swear she saw a satisfied grin beneath a crown of roses among the branches overhead, followed by a shimmer of rich blue velvet fluttering out of sight.

"The food, niña, now!"

Flinching at the impatience in Abuela's tone, Lina ran a light finger over Beltran's crest, easing off the goggles and cowl, and then gently shooed him from the basket. He fluttered easily to a nearby tree branch so she could draw out the pan de muertos, roasted goat, and huevos con nopales she and Abuela had prepared earlier for the oferenda feast. Once she'd placed everything to her grandmother's satisfaction, Lina removed her mask and goggles—storing them in her now-empty basket—and she and Abuela lay their weary bones down to rest.

Lina woke surrounded by obsidian darkness. Though dew-sprinkled grass had cushioned her body what seemed like only moments before, now she stood. The rough stone beneath her feet seared her soles like bitter ice, and the breath of the surrounding hills bit with the chill of death. The path, however, glowed with golden light scattered before her, here thick, there faint, but always steady, always sure. Kneeling, she ran her hand over the ground, encountering the soft crinkle of marigold petals. As they continued to glow against the palm of her hand, she knew she traveled the Land of the Dead.

Sliding the petals into the pocket of her robe, she continued, keeping her feet to that path lest she be lost, her gaze searching the craggy distance ahead for the beacon that drew her. The flutter of wings swirled overhead, but she could not see feather or form to know the nature of the bird. Or what she *hoped* was a bird.

A burst of wind speared toward her through the angular hills, focusing her thoughts on her journey. It carried a raspy whisper, *"Come, mija, come to me. We must have words between us."*

Shivers rippled across Lina's skin beneath her worn cotton robe, but she followed the beckoning, somehow both climbing and descending at once along the golden path, her senses whirling but never losing the thread of that whisper leading her forward. Ahead, a cool white glow teased the horizon, picking out the hilly peaks looming sentinel over the path.

In the surrounding darkness, the air smelled and felt dry as dust while the clatter of bones danced in clicks and clacks, echoing off stony mounds. Sometimes close, sometimes fading off. And still, Lina continued on, a lifetime of wandering in a single instant. Instinct urged her forward though her gut rebelled. With each step, the icy chill climbed higher, caressing her toes, and then her ankles, and upward to her shins. Her heart quailed that it should be caught in that cold and final grip.

Yet, Lina continued.

The golden glow she followed paled, suddenly enveloped by a surge in the soft white light, like moonbeams on burnished bone.

Lina's gaze relinquished the horizon to draw back, settling on the stately figure that appeared to stand before her, slender polished bone curving gracefully beneath a soft blue veil crowned by roses so deeply crimson they appeared black beneath the arch of the underworld, for surely that is where her path had taken her.

Lina's feet stopped without her feeling the cessation.

As she gazed in awe upon Santa Muerte, and not merely her reflection, Lina felt the flutter of wings beside her head buffeting her briefly as the wind of this place had not. She turned and locked gazes with Beltran. Lina gasped, her hand darting without thought to reach for the crow, gaining a peck for her ill manners. Was this a vision fed by this place, or was the sight for true? Lina could not say, but as she beheld the crow, she could not deny he—or the vision of him—watched her, his head cocking as corvids are wont to do, training one gleaming eye upon her, then the other, before giving a barking caw almost like a chuckle. The crow alit on her shoulder, ruffling his crest like the proud, cocky bird he was.

"Your eyes," she murmured in awe, her hand still raised, if respectfully distant from an actual touch. "She's restored your eyes..."

"Righting another wrong that should never have happened," the saintly figure murmured.

Lina turned away from the crow and settled her gaze on the death deity.

"Why are we here?"

"Because I wished it. And you answered."

Lina nodded, conceding the point, though Santa Muerte had not truly answered the question as intended. But having just been treated to a lesson in respect from Beltran, Lina merely waited in a semblance of patience for the creature of death and bone to speak her piece.

The glow from the goddess's ivory served well enough in the stead of muscle and flesh, a fair approximation of an amused grin gracing Santa Muerte's face at Lina's display of circumspection.

With a faint nod, the deity raised her hand, weaving her metacarpals through the darkness, the darting display of light and dark leaving impressions on Lina's mind like a shadow play depicting a battle.

"You have shown great courage, a strength of spirit worthy of any warrior of our people," Santa Muerte spoke into the silence. "As has your friend there. The two of you have done us a great service returning that demon to the underworld."

Lina shuddered at the mention of the creature.

"But more importantly, you freed a soul unjustly denied the afterlife."

Anger kindled in Lina's belly as Beltran's talons gripped her shoulder through her robe.

"Two died tonight, unjustly, *but you only brought one back.*" She set her stance and jutted her jaw, daring the deity to deny her claim, her father more important to her than her own self.

At Lina's challenge, embers flared bright in the pits of Santa Muerte's eye sockets as the luster of her brow dipped forward. "Make no mistake, niña, Vasco courted his death when he sought to breach a barrier he was not yet meant to cross. It was a kindness to free him to move on. More so than he deserved to reunite him with the love he sought so rashly. There are others even yet that do not enjoy that good fortune."

Lina frowned but grasped no point in arguing. It was, after all, that desire that had driven Papa like an obsession… guided his constant tinkering until he invented the spirit goggles in an effort to see into the spirit realm and reconnect with her mother.

Compassion softened Santa Muerte's expression.

"Do you have the courage to serve us, mija?"

The chill creeping up Lina's legs briefly surged through the rest of her.

Serve *Death*?

Her thoughts painted many pictures of what that might mean, projected in rapid-fire flashes across the landscape of her mind. Most of them made her heart quaver.

"Ahhh… *shshshshsh*…" Santa Muerte said, her fingers fluttering as if to shoo Lina's fears away. "Do not surrender your courage so swiftly. I do not look for a warrior to banish demons. I look for a guide both clever and compassionate, someone to usher the souls who have lost their way… or been blocked from it." She paused as if gauging Lina's understanding.

Lina drew a steadying breath and willed her eyes to relax from their widening.

"And so, I ask again," the goddess continued with a serene smile though she had no lips. "Have you the courage to serve us? Will you stand as Lady Death's angel?"

Icy fingers seemed to clutch Lina's heart. She would be a fool to think such service as Santa Muerte asked of her would always be so simple as just ushering souls. Could she commit her life to deal with the good and the bad of the spirit realm? There would be more moments like the night of Día de los Muertos and her confrontation with the damned soul who had stolen her father's body. But then she must also remember Papa as she had last seen him, the glimpse Santa Muerte had allowed her of his freed soul reflected in the mirror backing the oferenda, reunited at last with the spirits of her mother and her baby brother. To help such souls as these, how could Lina not serve? Abuela would never understand… but perhaps she need not know…

Beltran squawked and set his talons, fluttering his wings for balance as Lina abruptly straightened, then slowly nodded.

Santa Muerte reached out, and Angelina did likewise.

As their fingers intertwined, the glow surrounding them brightened, then flared, banishing the obsidian darkness.

Lina jerked upright out of slumber, her hands clutched in tight fists and her breath coming at a rapid pace. Abuela muttered and rolled away, surprisingly making no noise on her straw pallet. Closing her eyes, Lina lifted her face to the morning breeze as other families began to stir around them. After a moment, her breathing calmed, and her hands loosened.

From her fingers tumbled a slender bone, brilliant and white, with a subtle glow she only noticed in the corner of her eye. A finger bone. With trembling hands, she reached to pick it up again.

Not a dream, then, she thought. *Not a dream.*

The import struck her like a blow, leaving her again without breath. Gripping the finger bone tight, Lina rose quietly, her gaze searching the nearby trees for the crow. As if summoned by her thoughts alone—or possibly just her motion—he flew toward her, settling on a tall monument a few feet away.

"Beltran," she murmured, then shook her head. "No… no… a new life calls for a new name, don't you think? Something fitting to our calling…"

The crow cawed softly, bobbing in the jerky way crows did, then cocking his head to watch her from one newly restored eye.

Lina cocked her head back and stared at him a moment, then releasing a slow, even breath, she whispered, "Ujier… you are Ujier" — *Usher* — "and I am Angel, may we ever live up to those names."

With that, she slid the bone into the pocket of her robe, lest she lose it, drawing a sharp breath as her hand encountered flower petals. Shaking her head, she put the contents of her pocket from her thoughts and turned to the oferenda. Abuela still slept, and in the nearby woods lived those with no other home and little but what they could forage to eat. She took up her basket and placed the food inside, then wended her way beneath the trees until she encountered clear encampments to gift with her offerings. Above her head, Ujier winged through the branches, cawing in clear pleasure at his restored sight.

When she returned, Abuela had gone, leaving everything behind for Angel to manage.

Grumbling beneath her breath, she placed the now-cold candles from the altar in a line across each pallet and rolled them up, sliding them into her basket without filling it. Then she took the rest of the items from the altar and nestled them inside, glad to have already disposed of the food. The basket packed, she glanced around to ensure she had forgotten nothing. Content with how she had left the gravesite, she hefted the basket over her arm, took up her scythe, and whistled Papa's special whistle to summon Ujier. Or, at least, to let him know she made her way home. The crow would decide on his own whim if he joined her.

Wisps teased the corner of her vision as she traveled the path. Aether? Or spirits? Angel could not say, but given her father's goggles rested at the bottom of her basket, she found it disturbing to have seen either unaided. But then, it only made sense that Santa Muerte would equip her servant with the necessary tools to carry out her charge. Angel's thoughts went to the bone and flower petals in her pocket, and a shiver danced across her shoulders. What had she agreed to?

And how, precisely, was she to do as the goddess bid?

Angel still had no answer after the long walk home.

As she approached their hacienda, she frowned. She had expected to overtake Abuela on the road, but there had been no sight of her. Now that Angel was home, things felt too quiet, the air taut, as if waiting, the chickens still in their coop. She leaned the scythe next to the door and set her basket just inside.

"Abuela?" she called out. "*Abuela*, is all well?"

Silence rang as her answer.

With a huff, Angel searched from room to room, her nose twitching at a faint, sour smell she could not identify. The odor grew stronger as she neared her grandmother's closed door until Angel's stomach spasmed in protest. She swallowed hard and dropped her mouth open rather than breathe through her nose. "*Abuela*? Please answer me…"

Again, silence.

Angel raised her hand to knock but stilled, listening hard for any sound. At first, she barely noticed as soft tears trickled from her eyes. For a long moment, she looked down at the knob before reaching out to turn it. As soon as the door opened, little green flies filled the air.

"No! *Nonono!*" Angel cried as she rushed inside though she gagged and choked on the smell. She fell to her knees beside Abuela's bed, her hand reaching out to clutch her grandmother's dress. "No!" she sobbed, and then there were no words, only tears.

Angel woke to the sound of banging from the kitchen, echoed by banging in her head. She groaned and shifted, not knowing why she slept on the floor, or why her face ached, or why she could not breathe through her stuffed nose.

But only for as long as it took her to look up and see the lightly mottled hand hanging over the edge of the bed.

As the memories came crashing back to Angel, the banging continued.

Frowning, Angel scrambled to her feet and out of the room, her hands fisted and a snarl on her lips. With no care for silence, she burst into the kitchen, ready to battle with whoever intruded on her mourning.

She stopped stock still.

She swayed.

Abuela stood by the stove angrier than Angel had ever seen her before in life, and though she touched nothing, the pots hanging from their hooks swung wildly, banging against their neighbors as if some unseen hand tried to yank them down. As if her *grandmother* tried to yank them down.

"Abuela…" Angel whispered, her voice broken.

Slowly, the spirit turned, anger and fear and confusion darting violently in her gaze.

The pots banged louder.

Thickening tendrils of aether wreathed her grandmother's form.

Angel leaned her head against the doorjamb. "Oh, *Abuela*…"

The spirit remained silent, glowing shimmers trailing down her grandmother's cheeks like tears.

They stayed that way for a long time.

"Who will do this *properly* when I am gone?" Abuela's spirit wailed, the sound wispy and hollow in a way Angel hadn't noticed earlier at the gravesite, though clearly, Abuela's passing had taken place sometime just after Angel had left for the festivities nearly two days before.

Sighing, Angel rested her head against the door and tried to think. She had scarcely expected to begin her service to Santa Muerte so soon or in such a personal way. Where did she even begin?

With a firm grip on the doorjamb, she climbed to her feet, more conscious than ever of her rumpled cotton robe. As she tried to smooth it down, her hand brushed the pocket. She stilled. Held her breath. Reached into the pocket and pulled out the finger bone and a handful of marigold petals. Both glowed.

Could it be that simple?

Slowly, Angel approached her grandmother with her hand held out.

Abuela's spirit glanced down, clearly not comprehending.

The pots resumed their banging.

Angel groaned and thrust her hand forward before she could think about what she did.

Spirit and flesh intersected, and though the otherworldly items glowed even brighter, all else remained unchanged. Angel's flesh crackled with sudden, intense cold.

Giving her granddaughter a frigid look, Abuela retreated in a swirl of misty aether, not gone but no longer visible.

The barest of tears trickled down Angel's cheeks as she stared at the contents of her hand. A finger bone. Marigold petals. Both still shimmered with an otherworldly glow, though now muted. Somehow, they had to be the key to guiding Abuela's spirit to her rest. Angel slid the items back into her pocket before collecting the scythe and her basket from the entranceway and trudging into her father's workshop… *her* workshop, now.

She set her burdens to the side and firmly closed the door. Though none remained to care, she drew out her old tarp and tacked it over the doorframe as she used to do so Abuela would not know she worked late into the night, as her father had been inclined to do. The tarp helped deaden the smell, but not as much as Angel had hoped.

She moved to the workbench and lay the contents of her pocket across the well-used surface. Then she reached up and, one by one, drew her father's journals down from their shelf. In all of his studies of aether and the afterlife, there must be something he had learned that would help her.

A persistent caw from outside pulled Angel from her current journal. Her neck creaked as she turned to look, evidence she had immersed herself in her search longer than she'd expected.

Rising, Angel stretched the kinks from her back and shoulders, then moved across the room. With stiff fingers, she undid the latch on the window, then lifted the sash, pushing one shutter wide. Fresh air flowed over her, clearing her head—and the room—of the persistent stench she'd yet to address. As she stood there, breathing deep of the clean air, Ujier glided into the room. Showing off, he fluttered to his usual perch—as he had been unable to do just the day before—and began to preen.

"What do I do, pequeño?" *Little one.*

The crow made low, soothing sounds deep in his throat but merely continued to groom.

Angel huffed and returned to the journals, leaving the window open despite the growing chill as the sun set. Reaching over, she lit the oil lamp and continued to read until the oil was spent.

As the room fell dark and only moonlight lit her way, Angel settled on the cot her father kept in the corner and tried to sleep but found herself too weary to rest. Laying there in the overwhelming silence, Angel silently recited the rosary for her grandmother's soul.

Angel woke to bright light streaming through the window. And her grandmother.

Abuela stood over the cot where Angel lay, a scowl on her face and accusation in her gaze.

"I wasn't tinkering," Angel muttered sullenly as she sat up, hearing *'Aleta Angelina Fabricio!'* in her head, if not aloud. "I was trying to find a way to *help* you."

The ghost turned and disappeared through the still-shrouded door.

And the banging resumed.

Groaning, Angel flopped back down on the cot and squeezed her eyes shut as she wished she could close her ears. Silently, she cried out to Santa Muerte for help.

Perhaps she imagined it. Perhaps not. In either case, soft words drifted through her thoughts.

You have the key. Now you must find the door.

Angel's eyes snapped open, her thoughts focused. She scrambled from the cot and over to where the most recent journal still lay. All of Papa's research had been focused on peering across to the other side. Windows. Not doors. But windows—or some of them, anyway— could be opened. Under the right conditions, aether let one see through to the realm of the dead, as Papa's goggles had already proven, but looking through was quite different from passing through. It all began with aether, though, and thanks to the goddess, Angel could now see aether.

Everywhere.

It had taken her father so long to perfect his goggles because he could not see that essence, only understand it in theory. But somewhere in his books, she had read of the device he had used to harvest the aether that had proven the key to spirit sight. Fortunately, the journal had included sketches. Thumbing through until she found the entry she sought, Angel examined those sketches, then delved into the cabinets and shelves, looking for the infernal thing.

She would have immediately known where to look if she had been thinking clearly.

Under the circumstances, however, she felt she should be forgiven for her unclear thoughts.

She found the device on the shelf over the workbench, where two brass-studded leather cases that had housed the goggles resided. Climbing atop the workbench, she hauled the device down, taking particular care not to drop it, even as the ruckus from the kitchen unexpectedly grew louder. Carefully, she opened the case, removing a peculiar bellows-like object attached to copper condenser coils on one end and a small glass receptacle on the other.

"Oh… that will never do," she muttered, eying the chamber barely bigger than a thimble. While the size made complete sense given the purpose her father had intended for the aether, there was no way such a small amount would constitute a door.

Grabbing a graphite stick and a piece of scrap parchment, Angel began to sketch, visualizing an aether window and how such a mechanism would work. First, she needed two panes of glass between which she must trap the psychopompic essence. Second, a gasket to seal the panes, and third, a flexible tube to replace the thimble receptacle attached to the billows, which could then be fed into her glass-paned gas chamber.

It took several attempts once she gathered her materials from among her father's supplies. A gum-based seal proved insufficient on its own, but an outer barrier of melted wax held quite nicely, and likewise, a waxed leather tube appeared sound enough for her purposes.

In theory, anyway.

The structure held, and she'd engineered a simple wooden frame to hold it steady, but she had yet to engage the device. Humming in an attempt to drown out the banging, Angel engaged the psychopompic pump.

At first, nothing happened, but slowly an iridescent cloud formed between the precious sheets of glass. It swirled and pulsed and seemed inclined to take shapes, though Angel could not identify what those shapes were meant to be.

Finally, the chamber appeared full… almost opaque… with the volume of gas she'd captured. In theory, she had her door. Or a window, anyway, and were the two so drastically different in the end?

At her back, Ujier cawed.

She jumped as the crow soared to the top of the doorjamb and tugged the tarp free.

Angel gasped at the sudden influx of stench.

She really needed to deal with the body. But first, to save the soul!

On impulse, she began reciting the rosary once more as she carefully gathered up a fistful of marigold petals and laid a clear trail from her aether window to the door and then through it.

"Abuela," she called, but there was no answer, or any sight of her grandmother's spirit, though Angel could sense she hovered nearby. "*Abuela!*"

The house took on a sullen atmosphere.

"Who will take care of you when I'm gone?" Abuela whispered. Angel more felt the words than heard them as they wafted through the hacienda, filling every room with an expectant air.

"I will," Angel answered.

Her grandmother scoffed, and Angel felt it to her bones.

"I will," she repeated. "I *must.* You can't help me now."

Pressure built like a pending thunderstorm.

No grandmother would ever concede to not being needed, whether they could actually help or not. Angel's Abuela was no different. Thinking quickly, Angel raised the point guaranteed to soothe any grandmother's wounded pride. "You helped raise me well. Now… Mama is waiting. *Maximo* is waiting." She desperately hoped her words were not false.

The banging from the kitchen slowly faded to silence.

Abuela drifted closer, her form gaining definition as her "foot" connected with the marigold path. Scarcely daring to breathe, Angel closed her eyes and gripped the finger bone tightly, visualizing the window… *her* aether window sliding up.

Her eyes flew open as she heard Abuela gasp with joy.

There, framed by aether and glass, stood Maximo, his tiny spirit body bouncing with joy as he waited to meet his grandmother. Seeing Angel, he lifted his hand and waved.

More tears brimmed, though Angel could not believe she had any left. A smile tugged her lips wide as she waved back. Then she waited. For a long moment, no one moved, then Abuela slowly turned to glance over her shoulder, speaking the words Angel hadn't realized she desperately needed.

"I love you, mija. This isn't your fault."

Then Abuela stepped forward, and the aether flared, leaving Angel and Ujier to mourn in peace.

Rhymes with Lenore

Ef Deal

1.

"Bore. Core. Gore. Cellar door."

Like a nail scratching tin, the machine's voice bit through the thick air of the metalworks laboratory. Edgar glared at his friend Hogg and the foreign engineer who had saddled him with the infernal device.

"I asked for assistance. I asked for a means by which I might relieve the melancholia that has plagued me these past cold months."

"Ignore lore."

The rasp of the clockwork figure, corvid-shaped with an oiled bronze head, burnished brass torso, and shimmering plumage of rose gold, grated on Edgar's ears like a rusted weathervane. The bird blinked its glass eyes innocently. Edgar would have sworn it mocked him with a wink. He leaned his fists on the worktable to stress his displeasure.

"I asked you to assist me in applying Golding Bird's theories of electricity therapy for melancholia," he said. "Hogg, you were my boon companion at school. I thought you, above all others, could understand my plea. Instead of Golding Bird—" He waved derisively toward the automaton. "You made a golden bird! A raven, of all things. And it won't cease its prattling."

Hogg, a wiry, genial fellow, peered over the rims of his spectacles. "But I know how much you love Dickens, old boy. I remember your remarking on his talking crow, Grip. I thought it would bring a smile to your countenance."

"Deplore," the bird croaked.

With a frustrated roar, Edgar swept his arm across the table to upend the Raven, along with an array of retorts, beakers, condensers, and flasks, spilling their contents to the floor.

"Pour more?"

"And you betray my confidence by entrusting my commission to this French *demon!*" Edgar pointed an accusing finger at the slender figure beside Hogg.

Hogg approached warily and put a comforting arm around Edgar's shoulder. "I assure you, Poe, Duval is the foremost electrical engineer in the field, specializing in clockwork automata. The Raven is exquisitely designed to your specifications, old boy; the finest mechanical intelligence. Were you meticulous in its application?"

Edgar growled. "I am not mad, Hogg. Angry, yes, but mad—never."

The two engineers exchanged concerned glances. With welding caps so tight against their heads and the odd goggle-eyed mask that covered Duval's eyes, they looked more like hairless diabolical creatures conferring on the nature of Edgar's soul. The tiny laboratory above the ironworks floor, already a steamy closet thick with fumes from the foundry, grew even warmer in the uncomfortable silence.

The Raven preened its burnished feathers, creating a soothing susurration of sound like brushes on a cymbal. It ruffled them out and eyed Edgar with the smug arrogance Edgar associated with his *pseudo*-father John Allan, demanding results he had never explained to the young orphan he had taken in, punishing mercilessly when Edgar failed to measure up to his expectations.

"Chore. Abhor. Boor. Knocked to the floor."

It taunted him.

Duval examined the Raven, stroking its golden wings and tracing its claws with the delicate care of a nurturing parent. "Monsieur Poe, the Raven generates a very low voltage when it preens and ruffles, energy it stores and applies through the electrodes in its talons. This conduction of electricity should not have enabled the machine any further interaction than the mild therapeutic application you requested. How long did you expose yourself to the electrodes?"

Edgar flinched at the question, not for its unintelligible content but because it was the first time Duval addressed him, and he had not realized Duval was a woman. His collar tightened; his face flushed. He had unwittingly entrusted himself to a woman, the very cause of his melancholia.

One woman: his wife.

A year ago, Virginia's throat had burst a blood vessel, and from that moment, the shadow of mortality consumed Edgar's life apace with the disease consuming his beloved Virginia.

"More importantly, monsieur," Duval said, poking her face into his, "were you in control of your own mind when you applied them?"

Flustered, Edgar snapped, "I am in possession of my faculties at this moment, madam, and I resent the insinuation."

Duval pursed her lips. "Hogg gave you clear instructions on the application. I heard him remind you that the influence of alcohol or opium while undergoing this therapy would incur dangerous consequences."

Edgar dismissed her. "*Baah.* I recall no such instruction, and I would have you to understand I do not make use of opium or any such insalubrious substances that would interfere with the clarity of my mind. Such rumors of my addiction are but gross slanders. Nor have I touched a drop of alcohol for many months, as I promised my wife that I would remain sober so I may assist her in these painful days. Alcohol does not agree with my constitution."

The rude Frenchwoman took up a lamp and pressed closer to Edgar, studying his eyes. Steel grey pierced Edgar's soul, analytical, intrusive, unforgiving. Satisfied, she said, "His pupils are responsive, not dilated. We'll proceed."

Outrage at the flagrant temerity of the engineer in travesty pounded in his temples, deafening him. He pictured Duval strapped into the experimental chair with electrical and galvanizing apparatus so forcefully applied as to eject her teeth from her skull. He trembled, constraining his fury.

Hogg patted his shoulder. "Easy, old boy. What do you say we recommence from the start." He gathered up the Raven and stroked its head, eliciting a sweet hum as its rose-gold plumage excited electrical forces. Hogg indicated the chair, wired to both voltaic piles and Daniell cells. "Take a seat again, Edgar. Breathe normally."

Edgar complied, even as he said in confusion, "Recommence? Again? We've done this before?"

"*Before. Core. Even more,*" said the Raven.

Hogg strapped leather cuffs about his wrists. "Yes, old boy, we have."

"He recalls no instruction? Nothing of our first session? This memory lapse concerns me," Duval said, frowning. She placed her hands on his head, almost caressing him. "Petit mals, peut-être? An underlying condition may inhibit the current or redirect it entirely. Zut, we cannot risk damaging such a mind as Monsieur Poe's. So imaginative yet analytical, meticulous yet *sensible*."

So, the woman has a soupçon of femininity after all, Edgar mused. Such muliebrity belied her grotesque aspect—strong jaw, broad shoulders, and muscular arms like a brawler's, and the monstrous blood-red ocular masque.

Then Duval drew a lace-trimmed handkerchief from her pocket and pressed it gently against his brow. Edgar shivered at her tender touch.

"Mon Dieu, Hogg, it's so hot, poor Monsieur Poe is melting," she said, "and so am I."

Duval removed her welding cap, unleashing a dazzling aureole of luxuriant honey-blonde hair the deep rich color of true cognac, XO, not the cheap gut-burning stuff served down on 2nd Street.

Ah, thought Edgar, *perhaps not so grotesque.*

Resplendent, in fact. Radiant when she smiled at him. But how could such pulchritude embody a form strong enough to manipulate the forces required for the exigencies of engineering?

Duval then closed a collar around Edgar's neck, cinching it so tightly he gasped in terror. Duval cupped his chin and smiled reassuringly, once again an amalgam of maiden and monstrosity, aglow with all that was desirable in a woman yet with demonic ocular lenses ogling him with clinical indifference.

"*Adore aurore, eyesore.*"

The Raven flapped its wings, picked at its beak with a single talon, and fixed its glassy orb on Edgar.

"This is exactly what we did before, Duval," Hogg noted. "Is there anything we can do to augment the results?"

Duval shook her head. "Nothing more." Her hair shimmered like the Raven's bright rose-gold feathers. "We must replay the first session," she insisted. "His mind is clear. The effect is assured."

Edgar shuddered at Duval's gruff dismissal of his friend's question, turning her demon once again. Hogg had attended the finest engineering school in the country. Why was this French Xanthippe in control of the session?

Hogg bent down to grin into Edgar's face. "Don't worry, old boy. This woman has been wiring machinery since before you and I even entered West Point. Her erudition is profound, the powers of her mind all-encompassing."

Edgar didn't believe Hogg's claims. His oldest friend had to be lying. *The woman.* The woman had attached herself to Hogg, beguiled him, misled him, breathed her foul poisoned spirit upon the collegial brothers, sundering their bond of trust.

Hogg threaded copper tips of wires into electrodes on Edgar's cuffs and collar while Duval cranked a wheel, initiating the spinning of a series of discs. The air thrummed with electricity. The machinery crackled and glowed uncertainly, flickering, then flaring, then arcing in the incandescent essence of ozone.

Edgar closed his eyes against the flashing lights. Dizzied, he saw his beloved Virginia, her face drawn in pain, her eyes gleaming with tears. Then her eyes grew round, rounder, darker, remolding themselves to bulbous ocular lenses in a masque of red leather.

Edgar's eyes flew open. Duval held the Raven in her hands. A wired cuff wrapped each claw. The bright nickel talons sparked as the Raven extended them to reach—*for Edgar!*

Talons punctured his scalp and dug deeper, deeper into his brain. Hogg threw the master switch.

Galvanized, Edgar no longer felt his limbs. His vision swam. His lips tingled. His tongue swelled in his mouth. A flood of power poured through him, not in jolts as from a Leyden circle, but in a steady, buzzing, thrilling current stirring every thought, every memory, every reality, every symbol, every vision, every illusion, every fancy, every—

"Enough!" Duval moved in to detach the Raven.

"No—"

Edgar's hand spasmed. He caught Duval's fingers. Duval's agonized cry was cut short as the surge of electricity paralyzed her, binding and entwining the two into one mind.

Every formula, every diagram, every figure, every theorem, every chemical, every element, every metal, every pipe, every cog, every sprocket, every —

Hogg shut down the master switch. Every *everything* ebbed, but every detail of it remained. Edgar slumped in the chair, an inexplicable pleasure lighting his face.

Duval yanked away. "Imbécile! What have you done?" The harpy shrieked, gripping her burned claw in pain. Duval stripped away her demon mask and glared at him. Her soft grey eyes glowed with all the righteous fury of an avenging angel in all her ravishing beauty.

Blood trickled down Edgar's face like a loving finger tracing his features. Hogg removed the Raven and set it in Edgar's lap. He mopped Edgar's brow and cheek, then stanched the punctures with a cloth treated with an unguent that stung.

Edgar stroked the metallic gossamer quills of the Raven's wings. Its sharp nickel talons caught in the wool of his trousers and pricked his thighs. "Rose," Edgar murmured. "Your name is Rose. And I will treasure your thorns."

The Raven cocked its head with a whirring of clockwork within. It ruffled its feathers, aglow with an aura the color of Duval's hair.

Edgar met its gaze. "Rose Cognac." His eyes widened in comprehensive correspondence.

The Raven blinked twice. "*You're more,*" Rose said.

2.

"*You began with Monsieur Dickens' crow. Now it's a raven? Like me?*"

"'Crow' is such a harsh syllable," Edgar said. "A single stress. I want no stress. 'Raven' is far more lovely a sound, the liquid *r*, the sensual *v*, the lingering *n*."

"*Flatteur. Do you not fear the reader will think it a pun?*"

Rose's voice, remarkably musical, resonated beneath the high ceiling of Edgar's room, which the light of the single lamp on the desk failed to illuminate.

Edgar trimmed a quill. "'Ravin' mad,' you mean?" He chuckled. "No, they'll picture a stately bird such as those who guard the Tower of London. With the mien of a lord."

"*Or lady,*" Rose amended. "*Trochees are rather harsh. They sound more like Iroquois war drums.*"

"Not if you emphasize every other foot and tie the line together with internal rhyme," Edgar pointed out. "Once in SWEET November's AUR-a as I DREAMED of dear Le-NOR-a…"

"*Oh, dear, dear, no.*" Rose cawed a laugh. "*That is, yes, I see your point on the meter, but chère Edgar, this is hardly elegiac in tone.*"

Edgar gathered the nib trimmings into the rubbish bin beside his desk and wiped dust from the desktop. Only when his setting comported with his fastidious nature did he dip the quill in ink. "I see her as dark-honey golden. Bright as the sun. Shimmering. Radiant."

"I'm sure you do, chérie. But your narrator is in mourning. Lenore is gone. She may have been a radiant maiden, but his world is dreary, bleak. December, not November. The night, Stygian in its blackness."

Edgar rubbed his brow, then muttered under his breath as he wiped away the smeared blood oozing from where Rose's talons pierced his scalp.

"I'm hurting you. I can leave if you prefer."

"No!" Edgar drew a deep breath to calm himself, surrendering to the flow from the electrodes on Rose's talons. "No, I understand you. Mood. A unity of effect. If the day were bright, the raven would need no sanctuary to enter."

"Voilà, chéri."

Edgar put quill to paper and began again, his mind alive with more than electricity. Images arose like wraiths from the grave and slithered into words faster than his hand could inscribe them. If he missed a beat, Rose guided him aright.

"Why 'saintly'?"

"Assonance," Edgar replied testily. "Stately raven, saintly days…" Blood dripped along his nose and onto the paper.

"They were not so saintly, you know. Disease, violence, war, prejudice. Your so-called saints would have burned you for a witch, given your unearthly morbid visions."

Edgar bit his lip, but he kept writing.

"Gently, chéri. You've grown pallid."

Edgar laughed. "Good word. The *pallid* bust of Pallas." He blotted away the blood and took a moment to wipe his brow.

With a ratcheting sound, Rose pivoted at the hips until she bent upside-down to gaze into Edgar's face. *"Now the vessel with the pestle has the potion with the poison, but the pallid bust of Pallas has the bird with the word."*

"Don't do that."

"Trochaic octameter."

"Stop."

"The chalice from the palace?"

"Enough!"

Rose righted herself and fluttered her wings, gouging deeper into Edgar's scalp as she held her balance, driving electrical volts into the poet's brain. *"Saintly. Sounds biblical. Clashes with Plutonian."*

"They enhance one another."

"Quoth the poet."

Edgar grinned. "'Quoth.' Good word. Quoth the raven…"

Rose croaked derisively. *"I wasn't quoting anyone. I was only —"*

Suddenly, there was a tapping at the chamber door. Edgar jumped, wincing as Rose tightened her talons to keep from falling.

"Darling," came Virginia's lilting voice. "I know it's late, my love, but you have a visitor."

Edgar had no need or desire for visitors entreating entrance. "Who is it?"

The door opened, and in stepped Hogg. "I came to see —"

Hogg recoiled, his hand covering his mouth. He quickly closed the door before Virginia beheld the grisly sight.

"My God, Poe, what are you doing?" Hogg remonstrated, *sotto voce.*

Before Edgar could stop him, Hogg extracted the Raven's talons and placed the Raven on the corner of Edgar's writing desk. The thrumming that had sustained Edgar through his writing leached from his fingertips. Enervated from the sudden loss of energies, he sagged despondent in his chair.

Hogg lifted Edgar's chin to examine his eyes. "Once again, you ignore our specifications on the application of this procedure. Once a day, no more than thirty seconds, for the relief of melancholia, Edgar."

Edgar rallied himself to rebuff his friend. "I recall no such proscription. Fiend! I was in the middle of a session. You have no right to interrupt my work."

Hogg snapped his handkerchief out and cleaned the blood from Edgar's face. "*My* work demands that I closely monitor *your* work. And Duval's work is being abused once again. How do you not remember what I wrote down in your own notebook?"

Hogg picked up Edgar's ivory pocket notebook and turned to the page with his instructions.

Edgar looked beyond the page, unseeing. "Duval. Genius. Such a gift she's given me, a portion of her soul."

Hogg slapped the notebook down. "You could have killed her."

"She called me an imbecile," Edgar murmured, "but she glowed like a Seraph."

"Of course she glowed! You lit her up like a lucifer lantern." Hogg took up the Raven and wiped its talons of Edgar's blood. "Lucky for you, she is an admirer of your work, and she chooses not to press suit against you. Let me fetch a balm for those injuries."

"Balm," Edgar said. "One syllable. Nepenthe. Three syllables. That works." He reached for his pen again.

"*Is there no balm in Gilead?*" Rose prompted.

"Iambs," Edgar dismissed.

She fluttered. "*Drop the 'no.'*"

"Ah! Such a blessing." Edgar reached for the quill again.

Hogg stopped him. "Edgar, listen to me. Let me treat your wounds, and let us work together for another solution to your illness. I've heard of great success with nitrous oxide to raise the spirits."

Edgar barked a bitter laugh. "Raise the spirits? Hogg, if I could raise spirits, I would not fear losing her forevermore. *Raise the spirits!*"

Grief swelled in a sudden overwhelming wave. He hung his head and groaned.

Taking a chair opposite, Hogg gripped both Edgar's hands and spoke gently. "My dearest Poe, you must not mourn the dead while they yet live. You only tease your fancy into deeper shadows out from which your own soul may never be lifted. Pursue this experiment no more, I beg you."

"*No more,*" echoed Rose.

Tears filled Edgar's eyes. Hogg pulled him into an embrace and let him weep.

"I am haunted by the horror in this home," Edgar confessed.

"*Horror. Assonance but not rhyme,*" Rose observed.

"Death and torment tainted the whole of my childhood," he lamented. "Now, when Virginia and I have found such delight in one another's affections, cruel fate sunders us. When you plucked my muse from my brow, you took the only comfort I have known these many weeks. Where else can I find surcease from such sorrow?"

Hogg held Edgar at arm's length and spoke solemnly. "I will not leave you, and you must not allow hope to leave your heart." Hogg debated, his gaze flitting from Edgar to the Raven, before deciding. "Very well, if you insist on such comfort as this mechanical intelligence can lend, at least allow me to consult Duval to devise a more appropriate setting for the flow from the electrodes."

Edgar hesitated. He looked to Rose for guidance. She flew to his shoulder and perched, and sat, and nothing more.

3.

Edgar scanned the laboratory in no little confusion as Hogg fiddled with the electrical chair.

"Madame Duval?" he asked. "She refused your request?"

Hogg muttered under his breath. He reached into the pocket of his white coat and brought out a folded note, which he passed to Edgar. Edgar stared at it, crushed.

"Only this?"

Hogg shrugged. "Nothing more."

"But did she modify Rose?"

"She did."

Hogg pointed to Edgar's clockwork muse on the workbench behind him. Edgar's heart stirred with hope to see the gloriously golden, radiant Rose.

The Raven cawed, then gave a quiet, wordless croak.

Edgar read the words that juddered and tripped across the page in startling sentences of stern yet solicitous intent:

desire, dearest, dynamic, devoted, dutiful, deserving, dedicated, divine, diamond…

A smile directed the whole of Edgar's mien as Duval's expression of her compassion for his well-being restored to him the dazzling vision of the refulgent evangel.

Then:

disregard, disdain, dangerous, depression, demented, dysfunction, deplorable, dystrophic, dysphoria, dire…

Hope waned. Edgar's eyes glazed over. "Fiend," he whispered.

Said Rose, "*Prophet, chéri.*"

Duval, who had the power to restore him to clarity, to comfort him in his passion, to heal the unseen murderous shadows by the light of her radiance, had chosen instead to abandon him, as other friends had flown before. As Hope had flown before. True, Duval had sharpened, not destroyed, not dulled his senses. Since the application of her process, Edgar had gained acute awareness of all things in heaven and earth. He heard, too, many things in hell. All these his febrile pulse now pounded into martial trochees. A groan escaped him, a low stifled sound rising from the dark well of his soul.

"*Don't be mad, chéri.*"

Edgar grinned wildly. "Nervous I have been and still am, but why would you say I am mad? No, dear Rose. Listen to the trochees. Octameter. Assonance, consonance, internal rhymes. This—" Here he waved Duval's farewell note. "Possesses none of those, no more than I possess her. If this be madness, then, *yes, let me be mad!*"

Edgar touched the *billet amer* to the flame under a Florence flask and watched the ashes mingle with the sawdust on the floor, bidding each a soft farewell with bitter frown and bitterer scorn.

"We'll proceed without her, Hogg," he said. "Our golden muse has flown. Let's hope the brass remains." He took his place on Duval's powered throne.

Hogg applied the cuffs and collar, then set hands on Edgar's shoulders. "This must be our final assay, so I beg you, don't ignore—"

"Your instructions," Edgar finished. "Yes, my hearing's not diminished. And as Duval has admonished us, proceed just as before."

Hogg affixed the clockwork bird on Edgar's fever-dampened head, then cranked the discs and threw the switch that closed the circuits. Power arced.

Edgar sighed in relaxation, not forgetting the vexation that Duval's communication had incited, curse her heart! For despite apocalyptic premonitions she predicted, anguished awe she had inspired did enthrall him all the more. Memory sparked desperate desires to ignite once more the fires of the brilliant inspiration that Madame Duval restored.

Said the Raven, "No, no more."

"I decide!" Edgar insisted.

"No, old boy," Hogg said. "Resistance ruined previous applications. This time just enough, no more."

Vainly Edgar sought to stop his friend from separating him from his mechanical Erato. Hogg removed and cleaned the bird. Then he studied Edgar's injuries and, satisfied, released him from the chair. Edgar stood, shaking.

"Need a hand?"

Edgar demurred. He could not resist suspicion that his friend had somehow cheated him, denied him the full benefits that Duval had designed. But for all the doubts within him, he could not deny the rhythm and the play of words that coursed through his electricated mind. As the hum of engines died down and was silenced, Edgar's pulse beat out in trochees and internal rhymes.

"Hogg," Edgar said, "This time, it has worked. I'm certain."

Hogg, relieved, returned the golden bird while promising to monitor Poe's progress on the morrow. Edgar stroked the Raven's plumage—glistening, golden, radiant plumage. No, Duval's auroral presence still remained, to his despair.

Said the Raven, "*Come, mon cher.*"

4.

"*But at first, you called me stately.*"

"Not anymore."

"*Now I'm ungainly? 'Grim, ungainly, ghastly, gaunt, and ominous bird.' Chéri!*"

"Be quiet."

Edgar dipped his quill and tapped the overdraught into the jar of ink, then recommenced his oeuvre, grimly grinning all the while.

"'*Thing of evil*'? *Edgar, tell me, what has turned your thoughts against me?*"

As Rose Cognac hopped across the writing table, Edgar swore. "Just as Lucifer from heaven fell, so too, you wretched raven, you have fallen from my favor, and I'll heed your words no more."

"*Ha!*" Rose Cognac scorned the poet. "*Could the source of this disquiet be the note of admonition from that brilliant engineer? You're a fool if you imagine that electrical transaction somehow bound our souls to yours.*"

"You have no soul," he scoffed, then sneered. "We were more than galvanized. I saw the world through Duval's eyes. I saw the admiration she bestowed upon the work I'd done."

"*You saw Hope,*" replied the Raven, "*and you thought you'd found salvation, respite, kindness, and compassion, where before you had felt none. Edgar, listen to my clockwork, spinning gears, and punch-card logic. All I am comes from the heart of science. Only this. No more. Madam Duval is a genius, but her skills, neither nefarious nor divine, were meant to better your condition, nothing more. If you wish, I can depart, but if you'd rather, I'll impart what humble power I possess to ease your melancholy mind.*"

Edgar shook his head. "I've had enough of loneliness and dread, but I pursue it nonetheless to spite the looming shade of death."

"*You have let your sorrow fester into thoughts morose and desperate, digging deeper into melancholy with each waking breath. Let my gentle power ignite your senses to a path much brighter. With illumination comes the recognition that your love —*"

"Do not speak to me of love!"

Edgar exploded in a fury. When he gripped his hair to tear it, blood encrimsoned quaking hands. Edgar groaned and showed the Raven evidence of its remaining, all-enthralling power to control the poet's slightest thought.

"You can't blame me, Edgar. Since Duval replaced my circuits, you have not so much as let me touch electrodes to your fevered brain." Then Rose Cognac spread her plumage. *"You began this work as homage to the woman whom you wed and soon will lose, Virginia Clemm. Now your elegy is tainted. You've allowed yourself to wallow in a mire of maudlin doggerel. Edgar, listen, I implore."*

"A machine, and nothing more." Edgar seized the Raven roughly by the throat. "You dare insult me? When the goddess who created you admired what you disdain? My work you may find macabre, but my heart is black from harboring the horror of my future. You can't fathom such a pain!"

Edgar rattled his mechanical companion till her solder flaked and cracked. Rose Cognac cackled, cawed, and croaked in dire dismay.

"You prefer your pain!" the Raven shrieked. *"So, tell me why you seek to murder her creation with those bloodied hands you fold to pray? Is your madness so compelling you insist dwelling on darkness as the only way to purge these demons from your burdened soul?"*

But while Edgar frothed in rage, the Raven managed to engage her clockwork talons. Edgar yelped as fifty volts shot through his heart.

5.

Hogg found Edgar on the floor.

6.

October winds, cold and bitter, clawed at the tombstones, monuments, and markers in the west Baltimore burying ground. Their piquant spice of decaying leaves mingled with the fishy odors of the Basin's daily catch as they moaned their paean to the failing day, continuing their assault on the token memorials to the dead. Rainless, leaden clouds muffled the noises of the city, lending an insufferable gloom over the whole sorrowful thanascape.

Edgar turned his collar up and thrust his hands deep into his pockets with an icy, sinking sickening of his heart.

A guttural cry revived him. Rose Cognac swooped in on a providential gust to land in the long bluegrass knotted with sedges, chickweed, and bittercress, blanketing a depression in the ground. Edgar rose and offered his arm; Rose flitted up to perch. She rubbed her beak along his neck.

"You remembered," Edgar said.

"*Toujours.*" Rose hopped up to his shoulder. "*Mon amour.*"

Edgar gazed across the burying ground, tallying the marble reminders of so many notables, statesmen, men of honor, heroes of war. He dug his toe into the mass of weeds at his feet, stirring a cloud of pungent molds. He prodded out a rock upon which someone had crudely painted "80."

"*Four score. Wherefore?*"

"I don't know any more than you, Rose. The novels, the poems, the essays, the reviews, the tales of terror. What was any of it for?"

Rose nuzzled him. "Lenore."

Edgar closed his eyes. "My *tour de force.*" He bowed his head. "Now my name and reputation are slandered by adversaries, libeled by my contemporaries. I'm the stuff of mockery. I go down to my rest in mendacious infamy. Nothing more."

Rose shook out her plumage. Aglow with electrical forces, she hopped up to take her place upon Edgar's head. Sparks crackled and arced about her.

"*Once more?*"

Edgar gently removed her and cradled her in his arms. "My golden bird. My muse and mentor." He set her down on the blanket of over-long grasses and worts and laid himself out beside her, his hands folded over his heart. "Next year?"

Rose slid her beak across his lips. "Evermore."

As evening consumed the last of the light, enshrouding the burial ground in Stygian darkness, Edgar descended into his unmarked grave once more.

About the Authors

Aaron Rosenberg is the best-selling, award-winning author of nearly fifty novels, including the *DuckBob* SF comedy series, the *Relicant Chronicles* epic fantasy series, the Areyat Islands fantasy pirate mystery series, the *Dread Remora* space-opera series, and, with David Niall Wilson, the *O.C.L.T.* occult thriller series. His tie-in work contains novels for *Star Trek*, *Warhammer*, *World of WarCraft*, *Stargate: Atlantis*, *Shadowrun*, *Mutants & Masterminds*, and *Eureka* and short stories for *The X-Files*, *World of Darkness*, *Crusader Kings II*, *Deadlands*, *Master of Orion*, and *Europa Universalis IV*. He has written children's books (including the original series STEM Squad and Pete and Penny's Pizza Puzzles, the award-winning *Bandslam: The Junior Novel*, and the #1 best-selling *42: The Jackie Robinson Story*), educational books on a variety of topics, and over seventy roleplaying games (such as the original games *Asylum*, *Spookshow*, and *Chosen*, work for White Wolf, Wizards of the Coast, Fantasy Flight, Pinnacle, and many others, and both the Origins Award-winning *Gamemastering Secrets* and the Gold ENnie-winning *Lure of the Lich Lord*). He is the co-creator of the *ReDeus* series, and a founding member of Crazy 8 Press. Aaron lives in New York with his family. You can follow him online at gryphonrose.com, on Facebook at facebook.com/gryphonrose, and on Twitter @gryphonrose.

David Lee Summers became a steampunk in 1987 when he used a nineteenth century telescope on Nantucket to examine the evolution of distant pulsating stars. Since that time, he has published a dozen novels and numerous short stories and poems spanning a wide range of the imagination. *Owl Dance*, *Lightning Wolves*, *The Brazen Shark*, and *Owl Riders* comprise the Clockwork Legion steampunk series. His other novels include *The Astronomer's Crypt*, *Vampires of the Scarlet Order* and *Firebrandt's Legacy*. His latest novella is a World War II-era cryptid tale called *Breaking the Code*.

David's short stories have appeared in such magazines and anthologies as *Realms of Fantasy, Cemetery Dance, Straight Outta Tombstone, Gaslight and Grimm,* and *After Punk.* He's been twice nominated for the Science Fiction Poetry Association's Rhysling Award.

In addition to writing, David has edited the science fiction anthologies: *A Kepler's Dozen, Kepler's Cowboys,* and *Maximum Velocity: The Best of the Full-Throttle Space Tales.* When not working with the written word, David operates telescopes at Kitt Peak National Observatory. Learn more about David at www.davidleesummers.com.

Michelle D. Sonnier writes dark urban fantasy, steampunk, and anything else that lets her combine the weird and the fantastic in unexpected ways. She even writes horror, although it took her a long time to admit that since she prefers the existential scare over blood and gore. She is the author of *The Clockwork Witch* and *Death's Embrace* and has published short stories in a variety of print and online venues. You can find her on Facebook (Michelle D. Sonnier, The Author). She lives in Maryland with her husband, son, and a variable number of cats.

Dana Fraedrich is a dog lover, self-professed geek, and author of the steampunk fantasy series *Broken Gears,* which includes the Amazon bestseller, *Out of the Shadows.* Dana's books are full of secrets and colorful characters that examine the many shades of grey that paint the world. When she isn't busy writing or attending book shows and author conferences, she can be found playing video games and frolicking among the Bookstagram community (the bookish corner of Instagram).

Even from a young age, she enjoyed writing down the stories that she imagined in her mind. Born and raised in Virginia, she earned her BFA from Roanoke College and is now carving out her own happily ever after in Nashville, TN with her husband and dog. Dana is always writing; more books are on the way!

James Chambers received the Bram Stoker Award® for the graphic novel, *Kolchak the Night Stalker: The Forgotten Lore of Edgar Allan Poe* and is a four-time Bram Stoker Award nominee. He is the author of the short story collections *On the Night Border* and *On the Hierophant Road,* which received a starred review from *Booklist,* which called it "…satisfyingly unsettling"; and the novella collection, *The Engines of Sacrifice,* described as "…chillingly evocative…" in a *Publisher's Weekly* starred review. He has written the novellas, *Three Chords of Chaos, Kolchak and the Night Stalkers: The Faceless God*, and many others, including the Corpse Fauna cycle: *The Dead Bear Witness, Tears of Blood, The Dead in Their Masses*, and *The Eyes of the Dead*. He also writes the Machinations Sundry series of steampunk stories. He edited the Bram Stoker Award-nominated anthology, *Under Twin Suns: Alternate Histories of the Yellow Sign* and co-edited *A New York State of Fright* and *Even in the Grave*, an anthology of ghost stories. His website is: www.jameschambersonline.com.

Jessica Lucci is a poet and steampunk fantasy author who writes about modern issues while maintaining historic integrity. She makes her home in Waltham, MA, USA, with her time-traveling budgie, Lamarr.

Her poetry has appeared in *The Edible Anthology of Poetry Greatest Hits*, edited by Peter Payack, and also in *Lucidity Poetry Journal*. Her steampunk novel *Subton Switch* was a finalist in the 2019 Lesfic Bard Book Awards for science fiction. Other works include *Waltham Watch, Gustover Glitch, Salem Switch, Steampunk Leap Year, Steampunk New Year*, and *Steampunk Pride*.

Doc Coleman's stories have appeared in *The Ministry of Peculiar Occurrences' Tales from the Archives*, the Way of the Gun Bushido Western Anthology, the Steampunk Special Edition of Flagship magazine, and in the charity anthology *Paradise Found: Tales From the Library*. In 2017 he published his first novel, *The Perils of Prague*, the first book in the Steampunk Comedy/Adventure series The Adventures of Crackle and Bang. In 2018 he published *The Shining Cog and Other Steampunk Tales*, a collection of Steampunk short stories. In 2023, he plans on publishing the second Crackle and Bang Adventure, *The Kindred of Kali*.

Doc has been a perennial guest at Balticon, RavenCon, Capclave, and Continual. He is also known as a narrator and a voice actor.

When he isn't juggling projects, making a living, or mainlining podcasts, Doc is a gamer, an avid reader, a motorcyclist, a home brewer and beer lover, a fan of renaissance festivals, and frequently a smart-ass. He lives with his lovely wife and two cats in Germantown, MD.

Judi Fleming works as a training specialist and instructional designer for the federal government in her day job and thus much of her writing is of the non-exciting technical sort. She is a graduate of Seton Hill University Writing Popular Fiction Master's Program. Her stories have appeared in *No Man's Land, Best Laid Plans,* and *Dogs of War.*

Award-winning author, editor, and publisher **Danielle Ackley-McPhail** has worked both sides of the publishing industry for longer than she cares to admit. In 2014 she joined forces with Mike McPhail and Greg Schauer to form eSpec Books (www.especbooks.com).

Her published works include eight novels, *Yesterday's Dreams, Tomorrow's Memories, Today's Promise, The Halfling's Court, The Redcaps' Queen, Daire's Devils, The Play of Light,* and *Baba Ali and the Clockwork Djinn,* written with Day Al-Mohamed. She is also the author of the solo collections *Eternal Wanderings, A Legacy of Stars, Consigned to the Sea, Flash in the Can, Transcendence, The Kindly Ones, Dawns a New Day, The Fox's Fire, Between Darkness and Light,* and the non-fiction writers' guides *The Literary Handyman, More Tips from the Handyman,* and *LH: Build-A-Book Workshop.* She is the senior editor of the *Bad-Ass Faeries* anthology series, *Gaslight & Grimm, Side of Good/Side of Evil, After Punk,* and *Footprints in the Stars.* Her short stories are included in numerous other anthologies and collections. She is a full member of the Science Fiction and Fantasy Writers Association.

In addition to her literary acclaim, she crafts and sells original costume horns under the moniker The Hornie Lady Custom Costume Horns, and homemade flavor-infused candied ginger under the brand of Ginger KICK! at literary conventions, on commission, and wholesale.

Danielle lives in New Jersey with husband and fellow writer, Mike McPhail and four extremely spoiled cats.

Ef Deal is a new voice in the genre of speculative steampunk with her debut novel, *Esprit de Corpse,* but she is not new to publishing. Her short fiction has appeared in various magazines and ezines over the years. Her short story "Czesko," published in the March 2006 F&SF, was given honorable mention in Gardner Dozois' *Year's Best Science Fiction and Fantasy,* which gave both her and Gardner great delight. They laughed and laughed and sipped Scotch (not cognac, alas) over the last line.

Despite her preoccupation with old-school drum and bugle corps—playing, composing, arranging, and teaching—Ef Deal can usually be found at the keyboard of her computer rather than her piano. She is

Assistant Fiction Editor at Abyss & Apex magazine and edits videos for the YouTube channel Strong Women ~ Strange Worlds Quick Reads.

Esprit de Corpse from eSpec Books is the first of a series featuring the brilliant 19th-century sisters, the Twins of Bellesfées Jacqueline and Angélique. Hard science blends with the paranormal as they challenge the supernatural invasion of France in 1843.

When she's not lost in her imagination, Ef Deal can be found in historic Haddonfield, NJ, in a once-haunted Victorian with her husband and two chows. She is an associate member of SFWA and an affiliate member of HWA.

Levi Leland is an independent Edgar Allan Poe scholar from Rhode Island. He has specialized on Poe's ties to Providence and on Sarah Helen Whitman (the poetess from Providence to whom Poe was engaged for a brief time in 1848. Levi created and guides "A Walking Tour of Poe's Providence" that had a successful debut in 2021. When he's not studying Poe, you can probably find him sipping an iced coffee (like a true New Englander) and exploring old cemeteries with his Pitbull-mix named Ginny Poe. Levi is an amateur artist, historian, writer, and anticipates being an amateur at most other things in the future. To learn more about Edgar Allan Poe and Sarah Helen Whitman in Providence, visit Levi's website at edgarallanpoeri.com. You can also find him on Facebook and Instagram by searching "Levi Lionel Leland."

Virginia Poe read her first Poe stories when she was nearly nine years old. The Black Cat and The Gold Bug started it all for Virginia, picking them out all on her own in the elementary school library. Over the years the interest in Poe grew from fascination into a never-ending love. No matter if she is performing with her dance company, working as an MUA, or writing lyrics, all aspects of her life has been and continues to be shaped by Edgar and his works.

MOST STORIES END AT DEATH.

BUT SOME STORIES LIVE BEYOND THE OBLONG BOX.

Beyond The Oblong Box is a podcast born of a need to eliminate misinformation about Edgar Allan Poe.

Join your hosts Levi Leland and Virginia Poe as they discuss the loves, life, works, and the world in which Poe once resided.

https://beyondtheoblongbox.buzzsprout.com/

Our Poe-etic Patrons

A. L. Kaplan
Alicia M Rabb
Allison E. Kaese
Alp Beck
Andee Bowden
Andrew Hatchell
Andrew Kaplan
Anonymous Readers
Anthony R. Cardno
Aramanth
Ashley Grant
Asp Zelazny
Barb Moermond
Becky B
Bess Turner
Beth Kee
Beth Lobdell
Beth Rimmels
Beth Sparks-Jacques
Bill Kohn
Bodge Inglee Richards
Brendan Lonehawk
Brian D Lambert
Brooks Moses
Brynn
Buddy Deal

C.A. Rowland
Carl W Bishop
Carol J. Guess
Carol Mammano
Chad Bowden
Charissa D. Jones
Charity Myhre
Charlee Roth
Cheri Kannarr
Christine Norris
Christopher Hykes
Christopher J. Burke
Cindy Joy
CJ Frost
Colleen Feeney
Craig & René Arnush
Cristov Russell
Cynthia Radthorne
Dale A Russell
Dana Fraedrich
Danielle Ackley-McPhail
David Goldstein
David Zurek
Dayton Shaw
Deborah A. Flores
Debra Lieven

Doc Coleman
Don Crossman
Donna Marie Hogg
Doug Williams
Douglas G. Yeager
Douglas Yeager
Ef Deal
Elaine Tindill-Rohr
Elaine Yang
Ellery Rhodes
Elyse M Grasso
Emma Lombard
Eric Schumacher
Eron Wyngarde
Gary Phillips
Gavin
Gayle Homes Martin
Ginger Devaney
Greg Levick
Hadrosaur Productions
Heather L.P. Estep
Heidi B Pilewski
Helen Walter
Hiram G Wells
Ian Harvey
Isaac 'Will It Work' Dansicker
Jaap van Poelgeest
Jack Deal
Jacob H Joseph
Janet Worley
Janito V. F. Filho
Jason
Jeanne Talbourdet
Jeff Young
Jenn Long
Jennifer Eaton
Jennifer L. Pierce
Jeremy Bottroff
Jess
Jessa Willson
Jessi Sindel

Jessica Lewis
Joanne Burrows
Joe Monson
John L. French
John Shrek Walters
John Stuart
John Wilson
Jon W. Quigley
Jonathan Mendonca
Jonathan Roth
Jordan G Ritchie
Josh McGinnis
Julian White
June L. Chase
June L. Chase
Kal Powell
Kat James
Kathryn Black
Katie French
Kelly A. Durkee-Erwin
Kelly Pierce
Kerry aka Trouble
Kestrel von Nerdenheimer
Kierin Fox
Krinsky
Kristiina Mannermaa
Krystal Bohannan
KT Magrowski
Kurt Beyerl
Kyro Dean
Larien
Laura Pesula
Linda Pierce
Lisa Kruse
Lloyd Lively
Lorraine J. Anderson
Louise Lowenspets
Lynda McCann
Mad Madeline
Madame Askew
Madeleine Holly-Rosing

maileguy
Margaret Bumby
Margaret M. St. John
Mari Hersh-Tudor
Maria V. Arnold
Marie Devey
Marilyn Bennett
Marissa C.
Mark Carter
Mark Newman
Martin Oe.
Mary-Michelle Moore
Matt & Liz Aronoff
Maureen Lewis
Mel Follmer
Melody Huckins
Michael Barbour
Michael Fedrowitz
Michele Hall
Michelle LaCrosse
Mike Smith
Morgan Hazelwood
Museworthy Inc.
Natasha Hubbard
Neil Ottenstein
Nellie B
No Name
Oliver James Minall
Otter Libris
Patrick Thomas
Paul Mojzes
Paul Ryan
Paul van Oven
Phil Huffsmith
Phil Pearson
pjk
prophet
PunkARTchick "Ruthenia"
Rachel
Raphael Bressel
Rhonda Goodman-Gaghan

Rich Walker
Richard Novak
Richard O'Shea
RKBookman
Robert C Flipse
Robert Claney
Robert Dahlen
Robin Schwarz
Russell Dennis Trimble
Sally W
Sanan Kolva
Sara E. Ontiveros
Sarah Olliso Flores
Scantrontb
Scott Schaper
Sebastian Ernst
Shawnee M
Shervyn
Sheryl R. Hayes
Sioux McGill
Sonya Mota
Stace Johnson
Stacy K Waddington
Steph Parker
Stephanie Lucas
Stephen Ballentine
Stephen Buchanan
Stuart Chaplin
Susan J. Voss
Susan R Grossman
Tasha Turner
Taylor Hunter
tchwrtr
Tess DeGroot
The Creative Fund by BackerKit
Thomas Karwacki
Tim DuBois
Timothy Ryan Scully
Tina M Noe Good
Tom Tiernan
Tracy 'Rayhne" Fretwell

Valerie Bello
Vicki Hsu
Walter J. Montie

white beard geek
William J. Jackson

9 781956 463194